THE CASE OF THE
WITHERED HAND

THE CASE OF THE WITHERED HAND

by

John G. Brandon

RAMBLE HOUSE

©1936 by John G. Brandon

First published (GB) 1936
Ramble House reprint 2008

ISBN 13: 978-1-60543-096-6

ISBN 10: 1-60543-096-X

Cover Art: Gavin L. O'Keefe
Preparation: Gavin L. O'Keefe

THE CASE OF THE

WITHERED

HAND

CHAPTER I

ASSISTANT-COMMISSIONER OF POLICE (C)
IS A WORRIED MAN

IN a little restaurant just off Greek Street, Soho, run by a certain white-haired Signora Padoglio, Assistant-Commissioner of Police (C), Sir William Haynes, sat at dinner with Detective-Inspector McCarthy.

It was what might have been called an "unusual" place, the signora's, in no way vieing with many other much more ornate and largely advertised places of gastronomic entertainment in that truly Cosmopolitan quarter. The premises, which consisted of one extremely large room with kitchens below, had been for a considerable time run as a club, of sorts; that is if the appellation, "club" fitted a place in which knights of the sling-shot, race-course thugs, *souteneurs*, and the *femina* they preyed on, coloured gentry of occupations not to be specified, or even discovered, reigned supreme.

A razor-slashing affray had the result of the proprietor being hauled before the magistrate at Marlborough Street, from which place he was removed in a police-van, and the premises disbarred for use as a club for some five years.

For a considerable time it remained empty, save for the colonies of spiders which were reared and had their beings in the multitude of webs which, bit by bit, festooned walls, ceilings, and windows. Then, of a sudden, the whole of these latter were subjected to a generous coating of whitewash not to be penetrated by the eyes of the outer world, behind which things, to judge by the banging of carpenters and other similar sounds, were going on assiduously.

Then one evening at about eight o'clock the two doors around the corner from Greek Street were opened again, to reveal a large, spotlessly clean room, about which was set small dining tables covered with cloths as snowy as the walls themselves, and presided over by an elderly, white-haired lady whose name, to quote from the inscription over the door, was the Signora Maria Padoglio. Two young waiters, whose aprons were as white as the signora's napery, stood by, to attend instantly to the wants of such patrons as had the wisdom to take a chance and sample the signora's wares. Which, at the time of inspector McCarthy's discovery of the place, could be summed up in that expressive little word, nil.

His finding of it was eminently characteristic of him. Although born and bred in Soho and still living in the midst of what he humorously called his "clients," he had, for something like two months, been away handling with County Constabulary a murder in a Midland city. During which period the *Circolo di Romagna* had gone out of existence and the Signora Maria Padoglio's had, Phœnix like, arisen from its unholy ashes.

Back in Town, a stabbing affray which left a woman dead in a back alley off the Tottenham Court Road, had McCarthy on the run for the *Circolo*. His mind was miles away when, slipping through its double-doors, he stood amazed at the sight which greeted his eyes. The snowy cloths, the glittering cutlery and the sparkling glassware, the two pleasant-faced waiters who had nothing of *Maffia* or *Camorista* printed upon their olive countenances, and last, but by no means least, the white-haired lady in the little pay-box who bowed graciously to him, filled him with complete astonishment.

The Inspector, at a complete loss for about the first time in his life, conferred delicately with the signora. Did such and such persons frequent her most model-looking establishment?

He was informed that the persons whom he had named and also described with almost photographic detail did *not* frequent her establishment. Most definitely not. Furthermore, the Signora Padoglio had no wish, or intention, that they should do so. To begin with, the *Restaurant Padoglio* had opened its doors but the night before, therefore the signor would understand that of patrons of any kind there was, at present, a scarcity. Which, doubtless, by the grace of God, would be rectified in the very near future. The excellence of her food, as that of the wines which she was able to procure in the immediate vicinity, would no doubt bring about a complete metamorphosis in that direction.

McCarthy, in his very best Italian inherited from his Neapolitan mother, politely wished the signora a speedy consummation of her hopes.

But, that lady went on, not for a moment did she wish the patronage of such as the signor had inquired about—she had heard things as to what had happened upon these premises before; things, she assured him, which would only happen again over her dead body. Her desire was that the more respectable of her compatriots in the quarter (she was from Salerno, in the Campagna, she informed him) the tradespeople and so forth, would come to know her place, and her cooking, and would desire to eat the evening meal there. Possibly, also, the midday one—who could tell.

The very simplest and best of Italian food, the signor would understand, nothing not to be obtained elsewhere, but of a quality and preparation which should speak for itself. The signora wished that the signor might mention her to such of his friends who favoured Italian cooking, eaten in a simple, homely but without doubt respectable place.

The signor would. Moreover, being a hungry man at the moment, he, in the true McCarthy spirit, picked up a menu, studied a minute and decided that a murder off the Tottenham Court Road could look after itself for the next half hour or so.

Having partaken, for three and sixpence, of a meal such as he knew he could not get anywhere in the West End for double the price, plus a bottle of as good an Italian wine as could have been found in the Italian Embassy, itself, he assured the signora that if no other voice in the land was lifted in her favour, that of Detective-Inspector McCarthy would be.

He also promised her that, should any undesirables of the old *Circolo* give her the slightest trouble, she had simply to ring Vine Street and they would be given the very fullest attention without any undue loss of time. *Sapeti?*

The signora *did* understand—although he could see that upon perusal of a card he presented her with she was at considerable loss to understand a signor who spoke such perfect Italian having a name so evidently Hibernian as McCarthy. Which entailed explanation as to his Celtic origin on the male side, whereat the signora laughed and promised the Signor Inspectro di McCarthy the best of everything for himself or such patrons as he recommended, whenever he, or they, should honour her establishment.

Leaving the place, McCarthy put the word around, knowing perfectly well that it would go over the "grapevine" to every haunt in Soho within the next hour, that the Signora Padoglio's restaurant was *taboo* for such as could not remember the pretty manners their mothers had taught them at her knee. And, furthermore, that any looking for trouble in that direction would get it, full and plenty. On the other hand, such who were prepared to go and eat modestly, sedately, and like Christian people at the signora's, would do themselves no harm in his eyes. They might as well be in a respectable place for once in their lives.

But the mere fact that Inspector McCarthy, himself, together with friends known to be attached in some way or other to the dreaded C.I.D. had the habit of eating fairly frequently at the signora's was quite enough for the unruly of the tribe to give it a wide berth. Detective-Inspector McCarthy, although a most pleasant fellow, with an understanding of Soho and its denizens not usual among the fraternity of the C.I.D., was just hell on wheels when anybody got his goat. This was explainable to Soho by reason of his Irish father—Patrick Alysious McCarthy, Senior, who had, in his day, implanted wholesome fear of Erin in the Saffron Hill district.

And so it came to pass that upon this night it was at the Signora Padoglio's that McCarthy sat watching the worried face of his friend, Bill Haynes, what time that gentleman disposed of as good a dinner as ever a man ate with the air of one who didn't care a damn whether he had any dinner or not—in fact would rather not. From the Assistant-Commissioner of Police (C) was exuding an aura of gloom. He was upon the point of jabbing the point of a fork into the Signora's tablecloth—the joy and pride of her life, these—when McCarthy quickly intercepted the act.

"You'll pardon me mentioning it, Bill," he observed, "but if you want to die a sudden death just stab a few holes in the Signora Padoglio's cloths. She's a thrifty woman, and I believe she'd think worse of that than if you crashed the wine-bottle up against the wall."

Haynes laid his fork down with an obviously forced laugh.

"Sorry, Mac," he said, "but I'm that worried I hardly know what I'm doing."

"That fact must have been discernible to all and sundry from the moment you came into the place. In the elegant phrase of our American cousins: 'What's eating at you now?' "

"The same thing that has been for a deuce of a long time," Sir William returned with a sigh. "These eternal rackets."

"There have been rackets in London from beyond the day when Dick Whittington was Lord Mayor," McCarthy returned equably. "Which particular rackets are you eluding to?"

"The Vice and Dope rackets," Sir William answered. "They're growing daily, and we don't seem able to cope with them. There'll be a devil of a row before long."

"In fairness, Bill," McCarthy said quietly, "allow me, as a humble member of the C.I.D., to point out to its working boss that the first has nothing to do with him. Until some scoundrel or other is bumped off and a nice, juicy murder job made of it, the C.I.D. is not supposed to know anything of what's going on in that particularly

dirty form of crime. It's in the hands of the uniformed men, con-
trolled by a very capable Vice Squad from Vine Street."

"I know that," Sir William returned, almost irritably, "but the
Great British Public doesn't, Mac, and the Press, if they know it,
seem to forget it. Any more than we've anything to do with the dirty
foreign rats, male and female, who are creeping in here on forged
passports. That's the job of the Emigration Department, and our
men at the ports daren't say a word unless they're specifically
called in. That doesn't stop the public wondering why the Criminal
Investigation Department lets them get in, just the same."

"It's hard, Bill," McCarthy said sympathetically. "Divil a doubt
of it."

"So much for the Vice side," Sir William went on. "And the
Dope branch is getting still worse. The stuff's pouring in and we
can't get the slightest line of who's at the bottom of it. We're
picking up dope-runners in plenty, but never a squeak out of one of
them as to who are the big people behind it."

"What kind of dope in particular, Bill?" McCarthy asked.

"Every kind," he was told. "The West land's thick with it. All
the powdered drugs, and now opium as well."

"Getting the 'treacle' in, are they?" McCarthy said musingly.
"You'd think the smart lads of the Customs branch would be able to
get a line on that before the stuff's run ashore."

"They can't get the faintest trace of it, incoming," Haynes told
him, "but we know that it's being hawked, not only in London but
all over the country, in every variety of prepared form. But as for
where the main stock is, we're as far off picking it up as ever."

"Who's got it in hand?" McCarthy asked.

"Grey—Inspector Grey; the star in man of the Narcotic Squad."

"Heard of him, but never met him," McCarthy commented.
"I've been told he's one of the smart lads."

"One of the very best," Haynes assured him. "Rather like
yourself, inasmuch as that he's a 'lone wolf.' Likes to work sin-
gle-handed. However, up to now it's got him beaten as well as the
next."

"It's the divil himself how you can get up against the brick
wall," McCarthy said with a sigh of fellow-feeling, "and the worst
of it is that it invariably happens on a job that it's more than unusually necessary to make good on. Never mind, Bill, Grey'll
probably bring home the bacon before so long."

"We'll hope so," Haynes responded, albeit a trifle pessimistic in
tone. "If he doesn't, all Hell will pop before we're so much older."

He switched the subject suddenly.

"Let's see, what are you handling at the moment, Mac?"

"At the present moment," McCarthy informed him, "nothing worse than this good dinner. By gracious permission of the 'Sooper' I'm going to take a week-end leave. I'm invited to dance at a shivoo of Lady Featheringham's to-morrow night."

He grinned whimsically at Sir William's look of surprise. "I took such good care of her ladyship's and her guests' jewels at her last big affair in Berkeley Square that she's invited me as a guest this time. So, from now and until Monday morning, Crime will have to take care of itself so far as I'm concerned. I'll look in at the Yard in the morning for a few minutes, of course, just to see that no spectacular job has been pulled off to do me out of my week-end, but if all's calm and peaceful on the Embankment, Bill, I'm finished with work till Monday next."

CHAPTER II

IN WHICH A GRUESOME OBJECT COMES TO LIGHT!

TRUE to his promise, Inspector McCarthy dropped into the Yard the following morning and there reminded his grizzle-haired "Sooper" of his promise for a full week-end off duty—a concession grudgingly granted by his superior who appeared to regard it as an ill-omen.

"As soon as your back's turned, Mac, and you've got into those swagger evening duds of yours, something big'll break out and we'll be searching for you all over the place."

"It's myself that knows it only too well," McCarthy responded cheerfully, "but I'll take a chance on it. If I don't have one night off the prowl I'll be going nutty. Still, if it will be any relief to your mind I'm going to a supper-dance at the Florentine Hotel. It's just off Berkeley Square and you'll find the telephone number in the book. Lady Featheringham's party!"

The "Sooper" leant back in his chair and surveyed him appraisingly. Inwardly, perhaps, he was comparing the slight yet powerfully built figure of his junior, clad in clothes the perfect fit of which told only too plainly of their expensive origin in Savile Row, with his own, big, ungainly and shambling form, dressed in the one blue serge suit that no one in the red brick building upon the Embankment could ever remember him out of.

Perhaps, even, the comparison went as far as the good-looking, olive-skinned, dark-eyed and white-toothed features that McCarthy had inherited from his Neapolitan mother. All he'd ever got from the late McCarthy senior was a pair of hard-hitting hands, an inborn Irish love of a fight for its own sake, and a sense of humour that was liable to break out at any moment, propitious or otherwise.

"Damme, if I know how you do it, McCarthy," sighed the Superintendent. "You come here looking like a young duke whose pockets are running over with money, and you're dining here, and dancing there with Lord Who-the-devil and Lady What-the-hell, as if you were to the manor born. It must cost you a pretty penny, lad."

McCarthy grinned.

"I have to do something with the millions the State pays me for my services," he said. " 'Twould be criminal to hoard it up. And that reminds me, I have to let a little of it flow for a new dress-shirt as I go home, or else the beauty of the picture will be spoiled. Be the fairy uncle, 'Sooper,' and lend me a quid till Tuesday. If you do, I'll take the next few murders off your hands without so much as a grouse."

"That's a bet!" the "Sooper" snapped, as he produced the pound note. "You'd have had them, anyhow," he added whimsically, "but the good Lord forbid you should be seen abroad with a dirty shirt. It would be the ruin of the Department."

Ten o'clock that night saw the Inspector the life and soul of as gay a party as anyone would wish to attend. He was in the midst of initiating a dazzling young lady into the rhythmic mysteries of the rumba, when, from a hall outside the dance-floor, a telephone bell rang violently and insistently. McCarthy stopped and listened.

"I'll bet you anything," he said, a rueful hunch forcing itself upon him, "that that bell means Superintendent Burman is seeking the services of the gifted Detective-Inspector McCarthy. I have the feel of it in me bones."

As if to prove his sense of prophecy, an usher stepped into the room and up to him.

"You're wanted on the telephone urgently, sir," he said. "Divisional-Superintendent Burman calling."

"There you are," he grinned wryly at his fair companion. "What did I tell you?"

> " 'Tis the voice of the 'Sooper,'
> I hear him complain,
> You've been loafing too long,
> Get at it again!"

Excusing himself, he made for the corridor to realise as soon as he heard the quick, staccato tones of his chief over the wire that something really serious was afoot.

"Get to Fortescue Square on the run!" Burman snapped. "Make for Professor Farman's house—it's Number Nineteen. I've told them to hold everything until you come."

"What's wrong?"

"Murder—and worse than that! It's a Special Branch man, Jim Grey. Keep that to yourself, though. He was on Narcotic Squad duty."

"Grey!" McCarthy echoed, in utter astonishment. Only too quickly had Bill Haynes' pessimism in the matter of the dope-running been justified. "Do you happen to know what particular line he was on, sir?" he asked quickly.

"I've heard a whisper," Burman answered, "but it's being kept very 'hush-hush.' He was on a big opium-hunt, but keep that strictly to yourself."

"I will, sir," McCarthy responded.

"Get there as quickly as you can," the "Sooper" instructed. "It's in the uniformed men's hands at present, and I don't want them to get a chance of making some bloomer that will give us a devil of a lot of extra work and, quite possibly, muck things up for us altogether."

"I'll jump a taxi and be there within a few minutes," McCarthy assured him.

That space of time had barely elapsed when he jumped out of a taxi in front of a pretentious-looking house, before the door of which he caught sight of two uniformed men bending over an object huddled upon the ground.

"We had orders to allow nothing to be moved until you'd had a look at things, Inspector," a sergeant said. "We've kept the people of the house out of it for the moment, though they've been notified."

McCarthy knelt, and, in the light of the policeman's torch, examined the grey face that stared sightlessly up at him.

"How long has he been dead?" McCarthy asked the sergeant. "Any idea?"

The officer thought a moment.

"Roughly, sir, I'd say ten minutes. He was quite warm when I and one of my men found him. Luckily, there is a telephone just at the corner and I got through at once. I got my orders and waited for you."

"Do you happen to know his identity?" McCarthy asked quietly.

"Yes, sir. I've seen him several times about here."

"Keep your knowledge strictly to yourself," McCarthy cautioned. "That's important—orders from H.Q."

He turned the torch again upon the weapon which had unquestionably caused the man's death—a quaintly-handled knife, unmistakably Oriental, which had been driven with terrific force right to the haft in the dead man's left breast.

"Death instantaneous, I'd say," McCarthy commented.

The sergeant agreed.

"I'm waiting for the Divisional-Surgeon and the ambulance now, sir," he added.

"We'd better get him inside," McCarthy said. "This is some professor's house, isn't it? I didn't quite catch the name over the 'phone."

"Professor Farman's, sir. He's lived here quite a long time. I fancy he's a big authority on ancient things at the British Museum, but I'm not quite sure. I know that he goes there a lot. He tried to see if he could do anything as soon as we notified him of the murder on his step, and invited us to bring the body inside."

McCarthy nodded.

"We'll accept his kind invitation," he said, standing up and ringing the bell. "I'd like a bit more light than there is here. Wrap the body as closely as you can in your capes."

The door opened suddenly, and McCarthy found himself face to face with a tall, commanding-looking man whose features suggested instantly that their owner was a person of the highest intelligence. In some vague way the face was familiar to him; he was fairly certain that he had seen it reproduced either in newspapers or magazines in connection with scientific subjects of some sort.

"I am Detective-Inspector McCarthy, of the C.I.D.," he introduced himself, "and the sergeant has told me that you have been good enough to permit the body to be taken inside until the ambulance comes. I should be very glad to avail myself of that permission."

"Bring him in at once," the professor invited eagerly. "A dreadful business, Inspector. I should have been glad to do anything but, although not a medical man, I saw at once that it was hopeless."

Turning, he led the way through, and opened the door of a large room situated at the end of the hall and towards the rear of the house. It was as the dignified professor made his gesture towards the door that McCarthy for the first time noticed his strange physical disability—his left hand was artificial and covered with a flesh-coloured glove. From the freedom with which he moved his arm the Scotland Yard man concluded that it had been severed at the wrist.

The two uniformed men carried the body into the room and laid it upon the floor. The room was a veritable museum of smaller pieces of Egyptian curiosities, most of them, McCarthy judged, of great antiquity. There were carved pieces and statuettes of every description, and the walls were covered with friezes of stone and texture work depicting the life of ancient Egypt. There were photographs, greatly enlarged, of gangs of natives working upon excavations; in most of them was to be seen the tall figure of Professor

Farman. Although McCarthy took this in almost at a glance, the professor had noticed his interest.

"My life's work," he said, with a wave of his right hand about the room then, instantly, gave his attention to the still figure upon the floor. But before either he or McCarthy could speak there came another heavy knock upon the front door. Instantly the professor left the room.

McCarthy slipped his hand into the breast-pocket of the dead man's coat. He was anxious, in accordance with his instructions, to make sure that the murdered S.-B. man's warrant-card, which would inevitably reveal his identity, was not upon him. But he found nothing except a scrap of a torn envelope, upon which part of the stamp was left, carrying the last letters of a postmark, S-H-A-M. Absently he thrust it into his breast-pocket and went on with his search. It revealed nothing of any kind whatsoever, which seemed to indicate that the dead man had been searched immediately he had been killed.

Glancing up, he discovered that the professor was back in the room and on the point of addressing the sergeant.

"One of your men is at the door, Sergeant, and wishes to speak to you urgently," he said.

"Right, sir," that officer replied, and got up at once. "It will be one of the chaps that I left searching for anything they could find in the square," he informed McCarthy quietly. "Something may have turned up."

With a beckoning nod to the constable, he led the way out of the room, leaving the professor and McCarthy alone. The latter was turning again to the body when a sharp exclamation, which might have been either of surprise or dismay, brought him round. The professor was staring with excited eyes and pointing at the scrolled knife-haft protruding from the dead man's chest.

"Incredible!" he was muttering. "I did not know that there was another such in the country outside my own collection!"

"Another such what?" McCarthy asked abruptly.

"That knife!" the professor answered in a low voice which vibrated with excitement. "It is one of the very earliest forms of Egyptian steelwork. Those knives were previously in the hands of the Israelites during their first period of bondage. I have found quite a number in carrying out excavation work among the buried cities. Look behind you."

McCarthy turned, and, in a glazed cabinet, saw perhaps twenty weapons which, if not exactly similar, were extremely alike the one with which Grey had been murdered.

"Are yours all there?" he asked quickly.

One swift glance Professor Farman swept over the case, then nodded affirmatively.

"Nothing missing," he said. "The case, itself, is locked and the key is upon my chain. It would be impossible for anyone to remove one of those weapons from there without my knowing it."

He came nearer and was stooping as though to finger the haft, when McCarthy stopped him.

"Touch nothing, Professor!" he warned. "Nothing must be moved until the medical man has viewed the body."

"No, no, I understand that, of course," the professor said, drawing back. "It was purely my keen interest in the antiquity of the weapon which carried me away for the moment. As I said, I did not believe that there was another one outside that case in England. Beyond the recognised museums, of course."

McCarthy was just about to say that he would very probably have an opportunity of examining it later when, without the slightest ceremony, the sergeant burst into the room. In his hand, and with open distaste, he carried a gruesome-looking object which he pushed out for McCarthy's inspection.

It was, the inspector saw, a human hand which, years before, must have been severed from some wrist. The muscles had contracted, and, with its shrivelled, dark brown parchment-like skin, it was like some hideous claw!

"By the Great and Sainted Mike!" he ejaculated. "Where did this come from!"

"One of my men found it in the square half a minute ago," the sergeant told him. "Do you think it has any bearing upon this, sir?"

But before McCarthy could make any answer to that question, a hoarse cry came from Professor Farman. His eyes were fixed upon the ghastly-looking object, their pupils dilating wildly.

"Tell me," he asked in little more than a whisper, "are there two punctures—two black punctures—close together in the palm of that hand?"

McCarthy, although it nearly sickened him to do it, peered closely at the object in the sergeant's big palm.

"There are," he answered. "What of it? Have you seen the thing before?"

"Seen it!" the professor said. "It is my own hand! It was cut off twenty years ago by a mob of fanatic Egyptians who attacked me for what they called the desecration of one of their royal tombs. One of the ancient crones who was with them prophesied then that when I saw it again I could take it as an omen that I should shortly die!"

Fear, horrible fear, was in his voice, and his eyes dilated still more wildly with the dread that filled him.

"Has it come at last?" he muttered in a faraway voice. "Has it come at last?"

And before either McCarthy or the wondering sergeant could catch him, he reeled and crashed to the floor in a dead faint.

CHAPTER III

McCARTHY FACES A BLANK WALL!

"WELL," McCarthy ejaculated after he and the sergeant had lifted the fallen man to a couch and done their best towards restoring him, "this beats Bannagher, and, according to my old man, he beat the divil."

"Extraordinary business, sir," the sergeant whispered, his eyes fixed fascinatedly upon the grisly object he had hurriedly placed upon the table when the professor had fallen.

"Extraordinary!" McCarthy echoed; "No word for it. The most amazing coincidence I've ever struck in my life. A man killed at his door, and ten minutes later his own hand, severed twenty years before in Egypt, is found a few yards away. Add the prophecy of it, and it's enough to give any man the shock of his life. I know it would me."

He was about to continue his observations, when the sergeant, who had given a glance towards the man recumbent upon the couch, threw him a warning glance.

"His eyes are open, sir," he whispered. McCarthy turned at once to the professor.

"I'm afraid all this has been too much for you, sir," he said sympathetically.

Farman gave a weak inclination of his head and ran his tongue across his lips as though parched.

"Anything I can get you, Sir?" McCarthy asked solicitously.

"Nothing, thank you," came in a faint voice. With an obvious effort Professor Farman lifted himself from the couch and stood shakily for a moment. "It has been, as you say, a little too much for me. I have a restorative in my study that I think will help to set me right. With your permission—"

"Certainly, sir; certainly," the Inspector said quickly and moved to open the door for the shaken man. He saw the deep shudder which ran through the professor's whole body as his eye fell again upon that ghastly portion of his own anatomy mysteriously come to light again. For a moment he feared the professor was about to go off again, but by an effort he steadied himself and left the room.

"Yes, it's knocked the old gent, right enough," the sergeant commented.

"Not so old," McCarthy demurred. "And as for knocking him, I have an idea, sergeant, that if you, for instance, had lost a leg in the war and twenty years afterwards someone fished it out of a dust-box in your street and presented it to you, looking as that does, you wouldn't be so cheerful about it. I may be wrong, of course," he added mildly.

"Too dam' true, sir, I wouldn't," the sergeant agreed hastily. "And that's without the prophecy of being rubbed out when it *did* come to hand."

"Just so," the Inspector said.

A heavy knocking was heard upon the front door and the sound of a vehicle drawing up with a squeal of brakes.

"The ambulance," the sergeant exclaimed. "I wonder if the surgeon is with it?"

"Let's hope so," McCarthy responded. "If you open the door to them, you'll have first-hand information. Always a good thing," he added dryly.

But the Divisional-Surgeon was there, right enough—and inclined to wrath that he had been called away from a whist-party.

"I was dragged forth from a beautiful party, myself, Doc.," McCarthy told with him a sigh. "But there it is, the path of duty leads on to—I can't just think what, for the minute, but, in this case, murder. What do you make of it, Doc.?"

The medical man gave one look at the body, then almost snorted as he drew the weapon from the dead man's chest.

"What is there to make of it, except that a man's been stabbed to death with this thing? That's plain enough, even to—"

"Even to me," McCarthy interpolated. "Just about how long has he been dead, Doc.?" he questioned. "Approximately, of course?"

The doctor stooped and made further examination. "Not more than half an hour, I'd say."

McCarthy nodded: "That squares with the sergeant's statement," he said.

The Divisional-Surgeon regarded the dead face, frowningly.

"I seem to know this chap's face, somewhere," he said, puzzledly.

"Then should the knowledge return to you, keep it to yourself—outside official circles," he added significantly.

"Oh, then the identity's known?" the medico queried.

McCarthy gave an affirmative nod.

" 'S.-B.' man," he whispered. "On a very big assignment."

The doctor gave a low whistle: "That way, is it?" he said. Then his eyes wandered about the room.

"What the devil is this place. Museum, or something?"

"It's what you'd expect Professor Farman's house to be like, I'd say," McCarthy returned.

"Farman," the doctor exclaimed in surprise. "Not *the* Farman. Farman, the Egyptologist toff?"

"So far as I know, it's the same," the Inspector answered. "In fact, I'm sure it is. Pretty big bug in that line, is he? I'm not very much up in that sort of thing."

"Can't say that I'm altogether *au fait*, myself," the doctor said, "but I know enough to be able to say that, after Petrie, Farman's the 'big noise,' as they put it."

McCarthy jerked his head towards the door significantly.

"Softly, Doc.," he warned. "I don't particularly want him to hear himself discussed, even from that standpoint. He's had a divil of a shock, as it is. Laid him out for quite a while."

The doctor's eyebrows went up.

"He's not connected with it, surely?" he whispered.

"Not in the very smallest degree," McCarthy informed him very positively. "Except that the crime was committed upon his doorstep and he was good enough to allow the body to be brought here, he knows no more of it than I do."

The Divisional-Surgeon threw a side-long glance at the grisly weapon he had drawn from the dead man's chest, and another at the collection of similar knives in the case.

"That made me think that possibly—" he began when McCarthy cut him short.

"Nothing like it, Doc.," he said. "That knife is one of the curious coincidences of the case—that ghastly-looking hand is another."

The Divisional-Surgeon picked the withered hand up with the complete and total disregard of a man long inured to the handling of dismembered portions of human bodies.

"Pretty-looking exhibit," he murmured. "Whose is it, and how did it come here?"

In a low voice McCarthy quickly made him acquainted with the happenings since the body had been brought inside the house.

"God bless my soul!" the doctor exclaimed. "I've heard some extraordinary things in my life, but this beats anything in my experience."

He gave his attention again to the hand.

"What are these two marks here in the palm?" he asked. "Any idea?"

"None," McCarthy told him, "except that it was by them the professor identified it as his own."

"H'm. Look to me like the dried punctures of a snake-bite."

"Professor Farman gave no information what they were, or how they came to be there," McCarthy told him.

"Sticky business, altogether," the doctor observed. "Well, Mac, there's nothing I can do here. They'd better get the cadaver away. I'll let you know whatever there is to know that isn't apparent as soon as I can. But it won't be much I'd wager quite a bit. Or, perhaps, you'd rather it stayed until the finger-print men and photographers come."

"Their work will be outside the door," McCarthy said. "The death didn't take place in here."

"True: true," the surgeon acquiesced. "Examining him here made me forget that."

But for a long time after the body had been removed and the uniformed man had gone, McCarthy sat staring at two objects, each equally distasteful to him; the curved-bladed knife with which the murder had been committed, and the withered hand which had turned up again so strangely after twenty years. Was there any connection between the two—the murder and the reappearance?

He woke from a profound reverie to find that the door had opened softly and framed in it stood Professor Farman. That the scientist had steadied himself in some measure, was apparent, but if he were not still in a condition of frozen terror then Detective-Inspector McCarthy could not read the human countenance, which he flattered himself he could.

And, he noticed, the professor's gaze was not upon himself, but fixed upon the severed hand which he had claimed as his own.

CHAPTER IV

MURDER IN MISTAKE?

"WHEN you feel you're quite up to answering a few questions, sir," McCarthy said quietly, "there are one or two that it is my duty to put to you."

His keen eyes spotted that the professor was still shaky as he entered the room, closing the door behind him. He moved to a chair and seated himself heavily.

"I hope you're feeling better, sir," McCarthy asked solicitously.

"Considerably, Inspector, though it's been a great shock to me. You must forgive my momentary indisposition. The sight of that hand brought back memories; dreadful memories I'd hoped to forget. But I'm quite at your service now. Please ask your questions, and I will answer them to the best of my ability."

"The first," McCarthy began, "is have you the slightest idea why this man should be found killed outside your door?"

"Unfortunately, yes," the professor answered. "He had just left the house; indeed, I had only a moment before closed the door after him."

"Then he was personally known to you, of course?"

The professor nodded.

"Quite well," he affirmed. "A most interesting man, whose occasional visits to me, mainly for information, gave me the greatest pleasure. I met him first in the reading room of the British Museum. He was making a study of the various grades of Egyptian opium and the processes of manufacture. Like most men who have no actual knowledge of the country, itself, he was getting himself considerably tangled. I was able to be of considerable assistance to him."

McCarthy nodded understandingly.

"I took so much interest in his research," the professor went on, "that I invited him to come here whenever he chose and put any knotty problems he found before me. Poor fellow," he said with a sigh, "but for that mistaken kindness upon my part he might have been alive now."

"Did he ever divulge to you the reason for these researches?"

"He did. He confided to me that he was an officer of the Narcotic Squad of the Special-Branch at Scotland Yard. He virtually swore me to secrecy, and I can give you my assurance that his confidence has never been violated."

"I can well believe that, sir," McCarthy said readily.

"He further informed me of something that I had no idea of: that London was being flooded by vast quantities of Egyptian opium, which was being distributed all over the country from some point in the metropolis. He, I understood, was one of the chief men engaged in the suppression of this traffic. How true that was, I cannot say, but I believed him implicitly."

"You were quite right, sir," McCarthy said. "Grey was one of our crack narcotic men. Could you give me the reason for his visit to-night?"

"Yes. He wanted to know if it were possible for the seeds of the white poppy, from which all Egyptian and most other opiums are manufactured, and of which he showed me a packet of specimens, could be imported into this country and manufactured here. My opinion was that it could not, since the opium is distilled from the green or unripe head of the poppy, which would inevitably dry up and become useless in transit. If it were possible to import the green heads—yes; but those which he showed me were dried completely, and entirely useless for the purpose of manufacturing opium as we know it."

"He showed you those seeds?" McCarthy queried eagerly. "What became of them, sir?"

The professor looked at him as though surprised by the question.

"He took them with him, of course," he answered. "He had conceived them to be very valuable evidence against someone."

McCarthy's mind darted back to the fact that nothing at all had been found upon Grey's body. That looked as though someone implicated in the illicit opium trade had known that he was in possession of this evidence, trailed him to Professor Farman's house, and had killed him at the first opportunity, in order to recover whatever they thought incriminated them.

A tiny point occurred to him.

"You made no mention to the uniformed men who discovered and notified you of the murder that you were acquainted with Detective Grey?" he put.

The professor looked surprised.

"How could I possibly have done that, Inspector, without revealing to them the very thing he had asked me to keep secret—that he was an officer of the Special-Branch? The more so, as he had given me to understand that it was almost an essential that the ordinary constabulary should have no knowledge whatever of the Special-Branch operators."

"True; true," McCarthy admitted instantly. "You couldn't have said one thing without telling the other. That was a foolish question of mine." He thought again for a moment. "It's just a routine question, Professor," he began, "but I'd like to know the composition of your household—the servants, or any others you may employ."

"I have five menservants here," Professor Farman told him, "all Egyptian *fellaheen* who have been with me both at home and in my scientific work abroad for many years. They have no outside contacts, and none of them uses the opium-pipe—if that is what might be in your mind."

"It wasn't," McCarthy said frankly. "Did any of them know Grey?"

"Simply as an occasional visitor to myself. They admitted him in the usual way, but certainly none of them had the slightest knowledge of his profession."

"And these five Egyptian servants and yourself are the only people who live here?"

"With the exception of my private secretary, a young English lady, Miss Sophia Ridley."

"And she, I take it, is just an ordinary secretarial engagement from—from whatever place it is one engages secretaries?" he finished vaguely.

"Scarcely," the professor corrected. "Miss Ridley is the daughter of a man who worked with me in the East for many years, when I was conducting these excavating and other expeditions, more from the standpoint of making money than as at present—scientific research. Ridley was a man who had been everywhere and knew most things; moreover, he had a perfect genius for handling the large coolie gangs we were always forced to employ.

"He was a tough specimen, and, I am afraid, was scarcely up to the highest standards of moral conduct. But he was utterly fearless, and could get more work out of the natives of any Eastern country to which our enterprises took us, than anyone I've ever known before or since. He was a man of violent temper, and at times, indulged in fits of heavy drinking; so much so that, at length, we came to open disagreement and parted. He drifted somewhere East—up the Chinese coast, I believe—and I never saw him again.

"But when I returned to England to make a home and settle down to research work, I found out that, years before, Ridley had deserted a wife and child here. For the sake of our many past adventures together, I endeavoured to trace these dependants. The woman, I found, was dead; the daughter was being brought up in an institution. I undertook the care of her—she was then about sixteen—and had her education finished with a view to making her my secretary."

"Thanks," McCarthy said. "And where would this young lady be, either at the time that Grey called, or when you were notified of his murder?"

The professor shrugged his drooping shoulders wearily.

"That I cannot say," he said. "She has a small suite of rooms—a bedroom, a sitting-room, and a smaller office—in which she usually spends her evenings; I expect she would be there."

"Then the likelihood is," McCarthy said, getting up, "that the young lady is not aware of the murder at all?"

Farman looked at him a trifle dazedly.

"Since you put it to me, Inspector, I don't suppose she is."

"In which case, sir," McCarthy said, "it'll perhaps be as well to leave her in ignorance of it. There'd be no sense in unnecessarily alarming the young lady. Well, sir, thank you very much for the information you've given me. Some of it will undoubtedly prove useful."

The professor stood up, but to McCarthy's astonishment, did not offer to take the hand he had extended to him.

"No, Inspector," he said in an almost hushed voice. "It's not all; in fact, for me, it may be only the beginning—the beginning of the end! Without for one moment endeavouring to penetrate what may be in your mind, I would say that the suggestion to you is that this unfortunate man was killed by someone implicated in the opium trade which Grey was endeavouring, to smash. That is so, is it not?"

"Well," McCarthy replied, considerably taken aback by the direct question, "I've hardly given it thought yet, sir, but at the present moment my impressions do lean that way."

"In my opinion," the professor said quietly, "those impressions are quite wrong. I believe that Grey was killed in mistake—in ghastly and terrible mistake. The man who was meant to go to his death to-night was myself."

"You, Professor?" McCarthy gasped,

"Myself," Farman repeated in a still tone. "You heard what I said when that ghastly relic of my own shorn hand was brought in here? It was the fulfilment of a prophecy made by a fanatic old witch; a prophecy that will be followed up to its conclusion as certainly as night follows day."

"But, sir," McCarthy, "except in height, and, yes, breadth, there's no likeness between you and Grey."

"You remember how he was dressed, Inspector?" the professor asked.

"Of course," McCarthy returned. "Over his other clothes he wore a light overcoat and a dark brown felt hat."

"Exactly. Wait one moment."

He passed through the door into the hallway, leaving McCarthy staring musingly at the collection of ancient weapons in their glass case. A moment later the question: "Well?" turned him sharply.

Standing in the doorway was Professor Farman. He was wearing an overcoat of exactly the same cut and colour as Grey's; and on his head, and turned down exactly as the Special-Branch man had worn his, was a brown felt hat.

"Well," the professor repeated. "You realise the possibility now?"

"By heaven, yes!" McCarthy cried. "In that light, the mistake could easily be made."

"The moment I saw the knife with which he had been killed," the professor said sombrely, "and that, again, was followed by the return of the hand, I knew that the death dealt out to him had been intended for myself!"

CHAPTER V

PROFESSOR FARMAN REFUSES POLICE PROTECTION!

To say that the professor's startling announcement staggered McCarthy is to completely understate the condition of that young man's mind. Here, he thought, was a jumble up of a business that was enough to give any man all he wanted. And the result of questioning, put as delicately as possible to the elder man, did nothing whatever to simplify matters.

When at length he came out again into Fortescue Square it was, with a distinct feeling of profound relief. The aura of musty relics and dead men's bones with which Professor Farman's house was filled gave him the glooms, for one thing. A swathed mummy which stood in the hall immediately outside the doorway he had just left made him jump like a scared cat. He found himself subconsciously wondering how the young Miss Sophie Ridley got along with it all.

Quite apart from that side of it, the crime, itself, had got his usually acute brain reeling; it was, indeed, a divil of a business. Not because of its startlingly unusual and extraordinarily *macabre* features—they meant nothing to him, nurtured upon the unusual—but because of the brooding mysticism which seemed to hang over the whole ghastly business.

At first when he had heard of those poppy seeds, it had looked a fairly straight-line case: Grey had got too near to someone big in the dope traffic and had been put out of the way. That, in itself, though likely enough to be a job to turn a man's hair grey, was at least straight going, but on top of that there came this prophecy business put forward by the professor, and on the strength of what had happened, and the evidence of that withered hand, to ignore that was an utter impossibility.

That it had undoubtedly once been part and parcel of the professor's anatomy was not to be questioned. Then there was the ancient knife with which Grey had been killed, and of which there were several genuine replicas in the professor's collection. That a man of his scholastic eminence could have had anything to do with the actual killing was unthinkable, therefore it seemed sound reasoning to assume that whoever had committed the murder was also fairly well versed in Egyptology. And, again, it occurred to him, could have had sufficient knowledge of Professor Farman's collection, to know that it might implicate him to possess such a knife.

And last, but by no means least, there was that strange accident of Fate which had made the murdered Special-Branch man wear a coat and hat that night which was almost an exact replica of the one usually worn by Farman. All these things, either singly or taken together, seemed to leave no doubt that Professor Farman's theory that he had been the intended victim was correct. At any rate it was not to be turned down flatly as a figment of the imagination of a disordered, or at least frightened mind.

There was no sign of any uniformed men in the square, or of any of the police vehicles. The sergeant had evidently hunted his minions back on their beats with the departure of the ambulance, deeming, no doubt, that Scotland Yard could well look after itself without holding his men from their routine duties.

Around the corner he discovered a taxi-rank. At the moment there happened to be but two vehicles on it and McCarthy proceeded to question the driver of the foremost one as being the most likely to have been on the rank at the time of the murder.

"Were you here from about ten to ten till, say, five or ten past?" he inquired.

"Yus," he was informed curtly.

"Did you happen, by any chance, to notice any coloured gentry pass out of the square between ten o'clock and five minutes to. Hurry out, as a matter of fact?"

The taxi-man eyed him over before he answered. He was, McCarthy decided in his own mind, a cocky-looking young man—excessively so, in the Inspector's private opinion.

"Do you know these parts, guv'nor?" he inquired in the same cleverish tone.

McCarthy took a step nearer to him.

"Whether I do or don't," he remarked quietly, "is a matter for myself, not you. I'm asking the questions, just at the moment, and, if you're a wise young fellow, you'll answer them without any phlahoolic—if you know what that means?"

"Can't say as I do," came the terse answer.

"In which case," McCarthy said succinctly, "it'll be up to me to enlighten you. Phlahoolic, in the sense I'm using it, is damned impertinence, and let me have any more of it out of you, my lad, and I'll get into that shandradan of yours and you'll drive me as far as Vine Street; you'll get a whole lot more questions flung at you there and most of 'em you won't fancy answering, not a little bit. That is," he amended, "if I don't pull you down off that seat and give you the bum's rush there myself. Is the idea gradually permeating that thick skull of yours?"

"Blimey!" the driver exclaimed. "No offence, guv'nor! All I was wantin' to say was that if you do know this particular part, you'll know that there's dozens of these 'Indoo students livin' in boardin'-'ouses round 'ere."

"What I asked," McCarthy said with marked emphasis, "was whether you, personally, saw any of that colour hurry out of this square between ten o'clock and five minutes to that hour?"

"No, sir," the now quite subdued taxi-man answered. "I shouldn't 'ave took any notice of 'em if I 'ad."

"Wot about that bloke who took Jim 'Ogan's cab," the rear driver, who had been taking tremendous interest in the foregoing scene, chimed in. " 'E came runnin' out of the square, and 'e was a coloured man like this 'ere gent was askin' about."

" 'E was too big for an 'Indoo," the other objected.

"*I* didn't say Hindu," McCarthy snapped. "*You* placed the nationality, not me."

He turned to the second man.

"Give me a description of him."

Both, in chorus, agreed that the man was tall, well proportioned, and had an exceedingly hook-shaped nose. But the feature of him which appeared to strike them most was his inky-black, but brilliantly-glittering eyes, which were described as "ugly-lookin'."

Pressed further upon this point, they came to the agreed conclusion that "ugly-looking" was perhaps to be better defined as "wicked-looking."

"Them sort of eyes, guv'nor, that make you dodge a barge with the bloke they belongs to."

"Ah," McCarthy uttered, "now we're getting somewhere. How was the man dressed?"

He was, it appeared, clad, from what could be seen of them, in dark, well-cut clothes, but had a long overcoat, the collar of which was turned up about his ears and, therefore, made further observation difficult. But both agreed that he was a man of substance, and evidently in a hurry to get somewhere.

"Did you hear the instructions he gave to his driver?" McCarthy questioned eagerly.

They had not. But Hogan was due back at any moment to pick up a party of people in the square.

In exactly five minutes, Mr. Hogan and his vehicle returned. From that worthy McCarthy learned that his recent fare's destination had been Paddington Station. Which was all the information he could glean, save that he was an exceedingly free-handed gent and had presented Mr. Hogan with half-a-crown over and above what was "on the clock."

"Paddington, eh?" McCarthy said musingly. He took a cigarette from his case, felt in his pocket for his lighter and drew it out together with that small scrap of envelope he had taken from the murdered Grey's breast-pocket. In the flame of his lighter those four letters, S-H-A-M stood out vividly, but what town they referred to he had no more idea than the man in the moon.

Presenting his two informants with a generous tip for their information—which might, or might not, prove to be of any value—he strolled on, thinking hard as he went. His mind reverted again to the stricken, and undoubtedly terrified Professor Farman. He was sorry for that man. For anyone who had given their whole life to the cultivation of knowledge and science, generally, to be living eternally under the threat of a horrible doom was all wrong. And the worst part of it was that the professor, although he could not accept the situation philosophically, or even calmly, seemed to have made up his mind that it was close at hand. That infernal prophecy having come to pass with the return of his severed member, seemed to have established it in his mind that his end was not far off.

That anything of the kind could happen in London in the twentieth century seemed unthinkable, yet there it was, and no amount of argument could alter the fact of that hand. Additionally, Grey's death, garbed as he was, plus the spot at which it had taken place, was another thing that could not be talked out of existence. The menace was there, right enough. The professor should have police protection.

Obeying a hasty impulse, he made for the nearest telephone-booth and rang the house he had just left. He would have gone back himself, but it seemed to him a trifle indelicate to make another personal appearance there that night; it savoured of being too officious.

The professor, himself, answered his ring.

"I've been thinking, sir," McCarthy began smoothly, "that, after the things you've told me to-night—about the prophecy and all that—the best thing we can do to ensure your safety, is to give you a police guard. Nothing to be in any way obtrusive, of course," he hastened to add. "Just a man, in plain clothes, you'll understand, to follow on at a distance wherever you go, and keep a sharp eye out for anything, person or circumstance, that seems to him inimical."

"Under no circumstances whatever, Inspector," Professor Farman said flatly. "I realise the kindness of your intentions and appreciate them tremendously, but I have lived this long without being followed about by an armed guard and, even in these circumstances, I do not intend to begin now. And another thing," he proceeded in a less final tone, "I am, and always have been, a fatalist in such matters. Although the suddenness of happenings to-night shook my nerves to an extent which may have led you to think otherwise, that is the fact. What is to be, will be, Inspector; no human aid can ever avert the thing which *must* be. All that I can say is that it is my wish that you dismiss any such idea from your mind at once. Good night."

McCarthy found himself rung off.

"That be damned for a tale!" he muttered, almost angrily. "Courage is all very well in its way, but there are times when it can be overdone and become sheer foolhardiness. You'll have a man on your tail, whether you want it or not."

CHAPTER VI

THE MAN WITH THE PIERCING EYES TURNS UP AGAIN!

No man in this world was more stubborn than Inspector McCarthy once he got an idea into his head that a thing was right. Not even Superintendent Burman, himself, could get more mulish than could he. In McCarthy's opinion, if only for the credit of the Department, alone, it was essential that the murder already committed should not be followed up by another, possibly still more terrible. The professor should have his guard whether he wanted it or not.

With the object of putting this project into instant execution, he rang the "Sooper" and laid the situation before him.

"And I think," he concluded, "that for our own credit, he should not be allowed to have things his own way."

Over the 'phone, the "Sooper" "H'm'd" and "Ha'd" for a moment or two; McCarthy could almost see him rubbing that big prognathous chin of his.

"You believe the danger to be real and not imagined, Mac?" he asked dubiously. "I don't know much about this Eastern stuff, never came into contact with it in all my experience, but, to tell you the truth, it seems a bit far-fetched to me."

"All I wish," McCarthy barked back at him, "is that you could have had a squint at the hand they've already chopped off him. Perhaps it wouldn't have seemed so far-fetched to you then. And there's another thing. If I've got a good man tailing him, he'll report to me all persons who make any attempt to get near the professor, just who it is he's connected with in his daily affairs, and that will give me a chance to sort them over and find which one of them is likely to carry out this threatened job. Then I can nip him in the bud before he can make any start at it. Don't forget, 'Sooper' I've got a murderer to find, and one who makes a damned good job of it when he starts. And don't forget, as well, that there'll be a devil of a hullabaloo in the newspapers if a man like Professor Farman were killed at a time when Scotland Yard is investigating a murder committed on his doorstep."

"As far as I'm concerned, McCarthy," Superintendent Burman said wearily into the 'phone and trying to stifle a yawn, "have it your own way. You're in charge of the case and, if you think it necessary, I'm not the one to stand in your way. As soon as you're off the 'phone, I'll ring through and assign someone to the job."

"And put on a man," McCarthy warned, "who can not only jump to it, quick and lively, but hasn't got his trade plastered all over his face and feet—someone with brains."

"You've got the monopoly of those in this department," the "Sooper" growled satirically. "By the way," he added as an after-thought, "did you buy that shirt?"

"I did," McCarthy gave back, a grin upon his face.

"Well, all I've got to say is that I hope it wears well—and don't forget the pound on Tuesday. Now, ring off, and let me get through to put a man on to Farman and then get back to bed. Do you expect a man to be at it day and night?"

"No," McCarthy snapped back instantly, "I do not. And all I wish is that there were a few more up top that thought the same. Now that I'm satisfied that there'll be a man on the professor's tail, I'm off to bed myself—there's nothing more to be done to-night."

But, just the same, the last thing he did before turning in at his Soho lodgings was to write down the description given to him by the taxi men of the coloured man who had hurried out of the square at a time approximating with the murder, and who had been driven in haste to Paddington Station. The man who, though coloured, had struck them both as not being a Hindu, although the neighbourhood was thick with them. To this be pinned the fragment of torn enve-lope, then went to bed and slept as soundly as though no such thing as murder was known in this world.

Thus it came to pass that when Professor Farman, a bowed and shaken figure, passed out of Fortescue Square at eleven o'clock on the next morning, he had upon his heels a young gentleman who combined in his well-dressed person as astute a brain, coupled with a genius for speedy action and hard-bittenness as could be found in the ranks of the C.I.D. His name was Fox, and had he been called after that wily animal, his perceptions could not have been much keener, or his speed in an emergency much faster.

At the very moment at which he followed the dignified professor he was guarding to the British Museum and obtained a ticket which enabled him to follow up, still further, into that section entirely devoted to Egyptology, Inspector McCarthy was in conference with the Assistant-Commissioner of Police (C) Sir William Haynes, and Superintendent Burman.

Back and forward, they had already gone over every aspect of the case and, in addition, such reports as the murdered Grey had already sent in to his own Department. That the Special-Branch man had been upon the point of making a specific charge against someone in connection with wholesale Egyptian opium-running, seemed certain, but, with the man's native caution, he had never given the slightest inkling of the person or persons he suspected.

His reports left McCarthy quite as much up against the blank wall as did the mystery of his brutal death. Superintendent Burman, with a modesty most unusual in him, had frankly thrown in his hand on the job. As he put forward to the A.C., McCarthy had handled it from the beginning and had the grasp of what little there was to know. Moreover, mysterious withered hands, murder weapons a couple of thousand years old, and prophecies that might or might not amount to anything were a bit too much to ask a man of his years and avoirdupois to cope with.

"Let the inspector have all the glory, if there should be any to come from it, which I doubt," he said. "A bit of routine suits me better, these days. He can have my advice, of course," he added.

"Thanks," McCarthy said laconically. "It's good of you to give me the chance, 'Sooper'."

And although the Superintendent cocked his steely-blue eye at him quickly, not one sign of sarcasm could he see in McCarthy's pleasant face.

"For myself," Haynes observed, when Superintendent Burman had gone about his other business, "I incline to the theory that first struck you, Mac: The opium-running gang Grey was after had determined to remove him. In all probability they were tailing him for an opportunity and he gave it to them by going into that quiet square. It's quite possible that he turned into the professor's doorway with them upon his track, but was admitted too quickly for them to get him going in. They made sure of him coming out."

"That certainly looks like having been the way of it," McCarthy agreed, "but why do you say 'they,' Bill? Why need there have been more than one killer? Don't forget the information I got from those taxi-men."

"I don't suppose you've had time to go through Grey's athletic record, but I can tell you it," the Assistant-Commissioner said. "He was a first-class all-rounder and particularly hot with the gloves. As a matter of fact, one of the toughest men the S.-B. had."

"That only argues a tough scrapper," McCarthy disputed, "and don't forget that a man with a knife, particularly one who knows how to use it, has a big advantage over the other chap, no matter how tough he is. Particularly so if he makes full use of the element of surprise, as seems to have been done in this case. Now the knife," he pointed out, "is peculiarly the weapon of either the coloured man or the Latin. There's not the slightest evidence of any of the latter having been anywhere near the place. But there's no doubt whatever about the former."

"Ah, you're still harping upon this fellow," Haynes said, tapping McCarthy's carefully written-out *précis* of evidence.

"You bet I am," McCarthy said doggedly. "Have you pieced that description in your mind, Bill? I have, and it makes a powerful fellow. You add to that that he was lean-faced, and that says that he was most likely in hard condition. Then note that bit about his wicked-looking eyes, and that makes him a 'possible.' That's one side of it. Now, how did the hand which a reputable person like Professor Farman says was chopped off in Egypt years ago and which, he says, he has never set eyes on since, come to be in that square where the policeman picked it up? If it wasn't dropped by the murderer when he found that he had killed the wrong man and fled, then, in the name of the Great and Sainted Mike, will you tell me how it got there?"

The A.C. shook his head.

"It's a baffling business, Mac," he said worriedly.

"Baffling!" McCarthy echoed, "that's no name for it at all! I tell you, Bill, there's every bit as much to be said for the professor's theory that it was him they were after as there is for the one that the dope-running gang had got scared of Grey and wiped him out, and the place it happened at was just pure circumstance. I can tell you this—I'm damned glad the old chap has got a guard tailing him, and one who will jump into action without waiting to have his hair Marcelled on the way. I don't know why I call the professor old," he went on ruminatingly. "He can't be more than sixty, and of the lean, sun-burned type, at that. He's probably better than a lot of stout men of fifty."

"I've been looking him up in *Who's Who*," Haynes said. "I was surprised to find just how big a pot in his line he is. He's made some wonderful archæological discoveries, and has as many letters after his name as the Chinese alphabet."

"I wonder what it was they *really* lopped his hand off for," McCarthy said musingly. "He told me it was done by a lot of fanatic Egyptians for what they called desecrating one of their ancient tombs."

Haynes shook his head.

"It's possibly right enough," he said, "but, anyhow, the professor's the only one who could give you the right answer, if he wanted to. A lot of these scientific merchants are quite as fanatic on the subject of their own pursuits as the people whose royal tombs are being excavated. I've had a good deal of experience in the East, in both Army and police, and I've seen some terrible things happen through some of these tomb-opening, mummy-hunting professors. In their eagerness—you could call it greed in most cases—to lay hands upon these things, they seem to entirely overlook the point that the people they really belong to venerate them with an idolatry which is well-nigh impossible for the Occidental mind to understand. In my own personal experience of police-work in Egypt, Burma, and China, I've known of men whose deaths were reported to have been from malaria and kindred complaints, to die of totally different, and a dashed sight more horrible causes than that."

"Now that you mention it," McCarthy said, "he did say that once upon a time he and a tough member called Ridley ran these shows on a sort of semi-financial basis, which probably accounts for the severed hand."

"More than likely," Haynes said laconically. "What do you make of this S-H-A-M postmark, Mac?"

"At present, nothing. I've been running my mind over all the towns ending with those letters that I can think of, but I can't see any one of them in any way connected with opium-running. And even then," he added ruefully, "how the divil are we to make out which one of them it is. There's Horsham, Petersham, Melksham, and dozens more, all in totally different directions. It would take a squad of men six months to run the rule over the lot of them properly."

The telephone-bell at the Assistant-Commissioner's arm rang sharply. Lifting the receiver Haynes listened for a moment, then:

"All right, 'Phones, he's here. For you," he said, handing the instrument to McCarthy.

Grabbing it to him, the Inspector caught the voice of Detective Fox.

"The old chap is all right, sir," Fox reported. "He's chatting to a friend in the Egyptology section of the British Museum."

"How do you know that he's a friend and not some one who's perhaps forced him into an undesired interview," McCarthy snapped.

"Because they're as amiable as two turtledoves, sir," Fox told him, "and exchanging papers with writing on them. Another scientific gentleman, I should say."

"Quite possibly. What's he like—the friend, I mean?" Inspector McCarthy asked, not too interestedly.

But before Detective Fox had got very far with his meticulous description, McCarthy had stiffened up rigidly, and his eyes bulged almost out of his head. He grabbed a pencil from the desk, snatched up a piece of paper and commenced to write rapidly.

"Make it a full description, Fox," he ordered, somewhat unreasonably. "And make it accurate, too, d'ye hear me? *Accurate!*"

"I can't make it more so than I am, sir," Fox returned, a note of complaint in his voice. "What I'm giving you is as good as a photograph, sir."

"So much the better," McCarthy snapped. "Let it flow, man; let it flow. I think you're on something big. Height about six feet one," he murmured as his pencil flew over the paper.

"Weight probably between thirteen and fourteen stones. Ha! Does he look fit, Fox?" he asked eagerly. "That's a big point. Does he look a really fit man? Looks as hard as nails, eh? Fine! Splendid! Go on! Principal features an extremely decided hook-nose and very black piercing eyes." His head turned towards Haynes as he wrote on.

"How's that for the taxi-man's description, Bill?" he asked exultantly. "Go on, Fox. I was speaking to the A.C. Complexion coffee-coloured, and, when smiling, shows set of very white teeth. Yes? Dressed in dark tweed clothes, wears bowler hat, and looks decidedly prosperous. That the lot?"

"Tan shoes, and carries gold-mounted ebony stick," came to him over the wire.

"Right. Good work, Fox. Now listen to me, and make no slip-up. You get back to the museum and don't let that man out of your sight for one single moment, d'ye hear? Not for long enough to blink an eyelid. When he and the professor separate, stick to him and report every movement of his to me here at every chance you get. I'll arrange at once for a follow-up to tail the professor. And—mark this, Fox—until the two separate, be ready at any instant for the big fellow to make a sudden attack upon the professor. You've got that clear? Right. It may be by knife, or it may be by gun, but you be ready for any eventuality."

"And what's my line if he does?" Fox asked, an eagerness in his voice not to be mistaken.

"Bullet him!" McCarthy answered bluntly. "In the legs or anywhere else, not fatal. I've an idea that gentleman will be assigned to the nine o'clock walk before so long. Hop it back, man; back! Wait a moment!

"On second thoughts I'll make for the museum as fast as I can get there. But if by any chance they should separate, you stick to the coloured fellow. Right, hop back, Fox, and don't forget I'm depending absolutely on you!"

"Who do you think he's got hold of?" Haynes asked.

"A thousand to one the coloured man who rushed out of Fortescue Square last night and was driven to Paddington. At the present moment he appears to be hobnobbing with the professor upon friendly enough terms, but how long that will last remains to be seen."

"That hardly suggests him to be the man who tried to murder the professor outside his own door last night," the Assistant-Commissioner commented shrewdly.

"That's more than any man can say," McCarthy returned. "There's no game in the world where things are less what they seem than ours. I'll hop a taxi for the museum right away and try to get a line on our coloured friend."

He grabbed up his hat and made for the door.

"Make sure of a 'phone contact for me, in case anything goes wrong," he flung back, then disappeared without waiting for any reply. One stop only he made between that and Cannon Row, and that was at the totally inadequate cubby-hole in which he was supposed to work, and in which he grabbed an automatic and a clip of cartridges out of his desk.

But there was a second hold-up upon which he had not counted —that was in a traffic-jam in Holborn where he was delayed for something like six minutes.

When he arrived at the museum there was no sign whatever of the coloured man or his shadower, but at the extreme end of the museum railing, and turning into Montague Street, he caught sight of the erect, dignified figure of Professor Farman. He could only have missed the parting by a minute or two! What Inspector McCarthy said inwardly concerning London traffic-jams in general, and taxis in particular would, if uttered aloud, have got him six months' hard from any stipendary magistrate.

CHAPTER VII

IN WHICH McCARTHY MAKES THE ACQUAINTANCE OF THE BEAUTIFUL MISS RIDLEY

PROFESSOR FARMAN did not turn in the direction of his own home; instead, he walked through to Russell Square and took a taxi. For a moment or two McCarthy stood looking after him undecidedly.

"He'll be safe enough while he's in that," he decided, mulling over a "hunch" he had to take a look at the Fortescue Square house without the company of the professor. He had the desire, if it were at all possible, to give a little attention to the one female of the household, so far as he was aware: Miss Sophie Ridley. Certainly the professor had not mentioned any other woman, but had explicitly stated that he was served by five Egyptians who had been with him, both at home and abroad, for many years.

He hastened towards Fortescue Square and slowly sauntered around it, his keen eyes on the lookout for anything which might link up with last night's crime.

He saw that, by daylight, the professor's house was much larger than it had seemed to him the night previous; indeed, it was easily the most imposing residence in the square. From the opposite side of the railed-in shrubbed centre, he surveyed it, to discover that he was being watched from an open upper window by a girl, who, even at that eminence, seemed to have more than her share of beauty.

Judged from that height, she did not appear to be over-tall, but was certainly brilliantly fair and of that pronounced colouring which seemed to need no aid from make-up or the art of the hairdresser. This surely must be Miss Sophie Ridley, the deserted daughter of that tough specimen, who, if alive at all, was ranging about somewhere on the China Coast.

He did not more than glance up at her casually, but even that slight attention had the effect of making her move instantly from the window. He found himself wondering whether she had been acquainted of the tragedy which had taken place, for if that window belonged to the private suite of which the professor had spoken, and she had been there at the time, she certainly could have known nothing of what had happened.

As he moved along, he decided to take this opportunity of having a few words with this young lady, if it were at all possible. It was just on the cards that by a little judicious pumping he might glean considerable amount of information concerning the household which a learned *savant* like the professor, engrossed in one idea, could hardly be expected to give.

This idea, as well as his decision to carry it out, was strengthened considerably by the further discovery that the young lady was not the only one watching him from that house. From a corner of another window upon a lower level he caught sight of a brown-skinned face and two beady black eyes peering directly at him—one of the professor's Egyptian servitors without a doubt.

Promptly he slightly accelerated his pace, though not to such an extent as to destroy the apparent casualness of his movements. But, out of the corner of one eye, he saw that the brown-skinned man was still watching him closely.

Which started another idea: Did any of the servants know him for what he was? He had seen nothing of them the night before; the professor himself, having attended the door upon each occasion that it became necessary—with the exception of the police sergeant.

The thought flashed through his mind that it was just possible, not probable, but *possible*, that these servants might know something of the case. Many of the Eastern races, quite apart from the Chinese, were opium addicts, why not these? Entirely without the knowledge of their master, of course. The professor had been extremely explicit upon that point. He assumed that they had their own quarters in which they would be left entirely alone, and in which anything might happen without their master being in any way cognisant of it.

To build up a hypothetical case, could it not have been possible that Grey had found some connection between his Egyptian opium smugglers and the five *fellaheen* of the professor's household. And equally, although ostensibly he was calling to ask the professor's advice upon Egyptian opium, as that gentleman had informed him, could they not have had warning that he was there for the purpose of "shopping" them, and so killed him to prevent it.

But instantly McCarthy saw the weakness of that theory. To accept that, was to argue that he must have been killed before entering the house, and not after leaving it. Had he accomplished what he had gone there to do, the professor would certainly have mentioned it, instead of stating definitely, as he had done, that his servants were not pipe-addicts. And, anyhow, that did not account for the withered hand, or the man who had hurried out of the square at the approximate time of the murder; a man, by the way, whom

Fox's report had shown that Professor Farman was personally acquainted with.

He was still lost in cogitation upon this, when he discovered that he was turning the corner of the square and approaching a right-of-way which ran the whole length of the square upon the professor's side. He decided to take a look at the back of the house, though with no particular object in view. One last squint at the window showed him that the brown-skinned man was still watching him. Could it be that, although McCarthy had not seen him upon the previous night, he, from some vantage-point, had seen the Inspector and knew just exactly what was his official status. Otherwise, why watch him? Then it occurred to him that the man might be keeping a sort of general look-out on behalf of his master; the professor's way of endeavouring to discover if anyone inimical to him might be lurking about the place.

Almost the first thing McCarthy spotted when he gave his attention to the rear of the premises was what looked to be exactly the same pair of eyes still fixed upon him from a back window.

"A mighty good watchdog," he thought. If the other four were anything like as keen, an intending assailant would have a hard job getting at the professor, once he was in that house. The square, itself, was the danger-point, as it had been in Grey's case.

He found the back to be very much the same as those of the other houses, though, of course, larger and with the difference that two windows of one of the rooms were heavily barred.

That garden was enclosed by a brick wall, in which was inset a recessed wooden door, but, for the matter of that, the others were exactly similar. A long, slated-roofed outhouse ran the whole length of the grounds, and the apex of the wall which apparently formed its back, was fortified by broken glass set in mortar as, indeed, were the whole of the dividing and back walls. But, again, as most of the walls of the gardens had been treated in like manner, there was nothing to indicate any undue desire for privacy in that.

Retracing his steps, he determined upon paying his visit while he knew the professor to be out. As his rear exploration of the rear premises had taken up a minute or two only, it was scarcely likely that he had returned in that brief space of time. The mere fact of his taking a taxi at all, suggested either that he was going some little distance, or he had an appointment to keep for which he was late.

But before going to the house a "You May Telephone From Here" sign outside a small nearby shop caught his eye and gave him an idea.

Hurrying in, he 'phoned Haynes, to find out if, by any chance, anything further had come in from Fox. He was told that, so far, there was nothing.

"If anything should come in within the next quarter of an hour, Bill, get me at Professor Farman's," he requested. "And," he added, "unless speaking to me, personally, be extremely careful of what you say. The professor, himself, is all right, but I've been doing a bit of thinking on these Egyptian servants of his. Put to it, they might not stand the acid test. After all, it was Egyptian opium Grey was after, don't forget. I'm going to try to have a talk with the professor's secretary, this Miss Sophie Ridley."

Again as he entered the professor's front gate, he saw that those two dark eyes picked him up again instantly. His ring at the bell was answered by a stocky-looking Egyptian, whose face, in McCarthy's opinion, was by no means his fortune, and was rendered even less prepossessing than Nature had intended by what looked to be the cicatrix of a sword-slash completely down one cheek. The inspector could have sworn that the eyes which had watched him from the window were the same pair that were fixed upon him so sullenly now.

"I am calling upon Professor Farman," he began with his most amiable smile, to be answered by one terse syllable:

"Out!"

At this moment a door just inside the entrance opened, and he observed the beautiful girl he had seen at the window cross the hall. She eyed him curiously, but was keeping on her way when, with a quick movement which the Egyptian failed to intercept, he entered the hall and, hat in hand, accosted her.

"Miss Ridley, I believe?" he said, and, before she could answer, slipped a card into her hand. "I am really calling upon the Professor, Miss Ridley," he went on hurriedly and with a sidelong glance at the stony-faced and keenly listening Egyptian, "but I'd be very glad of a few words with you. My business," he added, with a significant glance towards the glowering *fellaheen*, "is strictly private and confidential."

Casting her eyes upon the card, she gave him a startled look, then led him to the room she had just left and closed the door gently upon them.

"You have come upon last night's affair?" she asked, a little tremulously.

So she had been made aware of what had taken place; so much the better for his purpose.

CHAPTER VIII

IN WHICH THE FIELD BEGINS TO WIDEN

DESPITE his engaging smile, McCarthy was appraising the young lady before him as keenly as ever he had done any unknown human quantity in his lifetime. If externals told truth, which sometimes they did, but, in his experience, very often did not, he was entirely satisfied with what he saw. If the parental Ridley had been as hard-boiled as the professor had indicated, he had certainly not bequeathed any of that dubious quality to his daughter. It needed no more than a glance to show that she was almost virginally innocent of the world, and that the crime which had been committed outside that house last night had shocked her immeasurably. The wide-open, even awe-stricken eyes with which she regarded this officer of a Law with which she had never come into the slightest contact, showed that.

"I haven't really come upon that particular business, Miss Ridley," he lied reassuringly, "As a matter of fact, I was just passing and thought I'd look in and have a word with the professor."

"I'm sorry," she said, "but what was told you at the door was perfectly correct. The professor is out."

A sudden thought struck her.

"How do you come to know my name?" she asked.

"Professor Farman happened to mention it last night," he explained. "He was giving me particulars of his household, and mentioned you as not only his private secretary, but the only woman in the house. At least," he added quickly, "that was what I understood him to say."

"You understood quite correctly," she told him. "I am the only woman here. My father was once the professor's partner."

"How is Professor Farman this morning?" he asked.

Her big eyes opened in surprise.

"The professor?" she asked. "He seemed perfectly all right. Why should he not be—except, of course, that he was greatly distressed over last night."

"Ah, well, now, that's the point," he equivocated. "You can never be too sure of anything after a happening like last night's. Who was the coloured gentleman who let me in?"

"That was Ali," she told him. "An old servant of the professor. He has been all over the East with him."

"Your father had been connected with the professor in the East, too, I understood?"

"Oh, yes," she answered. "For a very long while—at least, I understand so. Really, I know nothing of my father at all. He—he went away when I was only a baby."

McCarthy changed the subject quickly. "There are five of these servants, are there not, Miss Ridley?" he asked.

She nodded affirmatively and told him that they had all been with the professor for many years.

"They live, I take it, by themselves?" he put tentatively. "I mean that they eat and sleep and all that in a part of the house which is used by them alone?"

"I—I believe they do," she answered. "I think they use all the basement rooms, but I really can't tell you. I've never been down there myself—I have had no occasion to go."

"Ah!" McCarthy said thoughtfully. "You, I expect, eat in your own private quarters and do your work in the professor's study?"

"Oh, no," she said. Then amended the words. "That is, I *do* have my meals in my own rooms, but no one ever goes into the study except the people the professor invites there himself, and they are very, very few. No more than half a dozen, I should say, in the course of the year, and then only the same people. That room is taboo, and the museum as well; both are kept locked. Even when the professor is at work, he turns the key upon himself."

"How extraordinary!" McCarthy exclaimed.

"You wouldn't say so if you knew how he has to concentrate upon his work," she explained. "You can have no possible idea how frightfully difficult the hieroglyphics of the ancient parchments are to translate. Sometimes even one of them means months and months of work."

"I can well believe that," McCarthy said. "A very little of them would go a long, long way with me. And this museum is locked up as well, you say, Miss Ridley?"

"Always," she answered with finality. "Would you believe that in the two years since I came from college to become the professor's secretary I've never been actually inside it once."

"And just what does 'actually' mean, Miss Ridley?" McCarthy asked, wondering at the stress the girl had laid upon the word.

"Why, upon the one occasion that I can remember, the door was left partially open, I caught a glimpse, in passing, of the rows of mummies in their cases and the Chaldaic friezes which are to be left to the nation at the professor's death."

"They're not pretty things, mummies," McCarthy said, thinking with aversion of the hideous head of the one in the hall.

"No," she agreed with a charming smile, "I'm often glad that I don't have to work among them as the professor does. But, of course, to him, they're the most fascinating things in the world; those and the parchments and friezes."

"It's more than they are to me," McCarthy returned with a wry smile. "He's welcome to them for my part. I wouldn't work among them for a fortune, if anyone would give it to me. I suppose, then, that his study is near the museum?"

"It has a door which opens into it, I believe," she answered, "but I really don't know with any certainty because, as I've told you, I've never been inside either of them. They are the two Bluebeard's Chambers of the house," she added with a whimsical smile.

Some further talk passed between them in which McCarthy gleaned literally nothing of the slightest interest to him in connection with the murder of the night before, save, perhaps, one thing: that if ever a man's vocation was genuine enough from the standpoint of police inquiry, it was that of Professor Farman. The man's whole life, day and night, might well be encompassed in one word—research; more research, and still more on top of that.

But he also gathered that the professor's beautiful secretary had a pretty lonely time of it amongst it all. She had no friends to either come to see her, or whom she could visit. The professor, completely absorbed in his work, though kindness itself to her during the hours in which she assisted him, seemed to have no realisation that companionship was in any way necessary for her, or that she felt the loss of it.

"I often go for long walks about the City at night," she told him. "When the professor has locked himself up in his study for the night there's nothing for me to do, and sitting up in my own room, comfortable as it is, is apt to get very boring."

"You go alone?" McCarthy asked dubiously.

"Why, of course," she told him. "Who is there to accompany me?"

"True," he said. "I was forgetting that, for the moment. But I'm not so sure that it's the safest thing for you to do," he went on. "London is no worse than other big cities, Miss Ridley, but just about this particular part that you live there are a good many people whose ideas aren't altogether English upon the question of accosting unescorted young ladies."

Of his own professional knowledge, he could have made it considerably stronger than that. He could have told her that, inside the confines of Bloomsbury were, leavened amongst eminently-respectable citizens, about as dirty a gang of prowlers as could be found anywhere under the night sky; men well-known to the police to be connected with the infamous white-slave traffic, yet against whom no definite evidence had ever been procurable.

But since these night walks seemed to be the only pleasure or recreation in the young girl's life, he had no wish to scare her out of them, and, indeed, looking into those frank, innocent eyes, he wondered very much if she would have the faintest idea as to what it was he was trying to warn her against. But he made mental note to give the D. and other divisional men on duty in the vicinity the tip to keep a sharp eye out for her and to move swiftly in any case of molestation. This was still in his mind, when the telephone bell in the hall rang out sharply.

Instantly he jumped to his feet.

"Would you be kind enough to take that call personally, and quickly?" he begged. "It may be for me; indeed, I think that it is. I left word at—at a certain place—that I might possibly be found here for a quarter of an hour, or so. Just in case of an emergency, you understand?"

The big, violet-blue eyes fastened upon him reproachfully.

"I thought I understood you to say that you just happened to be passing and looked in," she said.

"Please take the call," he begged. "We can discuss that part of it later."

In a moment she had returned, telling him that his surmise *was* correct, the call was for him. Under the sullen, watchful eyes of the Egyptian, Ali, he answered it.

It was from Haynes.

"Fox has just 'phoned in," the Assistant-Commissioner informed him, "to say that your man made straight for that dive of Joe Raffi's off Shaftesbury Avenue after parting with Professor Farman, and that he's still there. He's closeted with Raffi in that office at the back of the restaurant—as he has the gall to call it."

It took McCarthy all he knew not to let out an exclamation of surprise. If there was any one thing more than another calculated to put a man in the black books of Scotland Yard in general, and McCarthy in particular, it was an intimate acquaintance with that unhung Sicilian scoundrel, the Signor Joseph Raffi. Only those black, smouldering eyes watching him, prevented him from opening up upon the subject of Joe Raffi, and anyone sufficiently friendly with him to be admitted to that back office.

"Thanks, he said laconically, hoping to the lord Haynes would understand, "I'll attend to it at once."

Before Haynes could say anything further, he rang off, and, a moment or two later, had left the house and was making his way by taxi in the direction of Raffi's notorious "restaurant" and night-club.

"I've yet to learn who our coloured friend is," he murmured to himself as he went along, "but the fact that he does business of any kind with Raffi doesn't speak any too well for him. Joseph is going to tell me who his friend is or trouble is going to drop upon the back of his greasy neck before he's so much older!"

CHAPTER IX

IN WHICH DETECTIVE FOX OBEYED ORDERS—
AND WHAT CAME OF IT

RAFFI'S *Café di Villarosa* (named after the town in Sicily from which the unspeakable Joseph hailed) was one of those irritant plague-spots to the Yard which they would have dearly liked to close down, once and for all. The very mention of its name to Superintendent Burman was enough to send that worthy officer into an apoplectic fit from sheer rage. The hours of his own time, not to mention those of his men, he had wasted over the place, gnawed at his very vitals every time the subject came into his mind.

The Yard knew that the dive, although frequented equally by the "Bright Young Things" of Society, and also by other "*Not*-so Bright Young Things" who had never even heard of Debrett, or Burke's Peerage, was a clearinghouse for "dry" dope—cocaine, morphine, heroin, and other kindred and equally deadly powders. They knew it beyond any question of doubt, but so clever was the signor that, never once, had they been able to get the evidence on Raffi which would have put that gentleman in the dock. The place had been watched for weeks and weeks at a time, both inside and out, but although some of the keenest men in the game had been assigned to the job, never one incriminating packet had been actually seen to change hands.

Yet there was no question that the "stuff" had been passed, and right under the eyes of the watchers. Young women who had entered the place listless, dejected, and only too evidently in that horrible state caused by enforced abstinence from the drug they craved, had been noted, within a few moments, to buck up amazingly and a feverish vivacity take the place of dejection. That meant only one thing—their craving had been satisfied.

Some of the cleverest women in the service of the Department had attempted with every trick of femininity to make good where their male coadjutators had failed, but without the slightest avail. Raffi still went about the place puffing enormous and expensive cigars, and laughed in the very faces of the police.

He was a big man, Raffi; not tall, but of that thickly-set and powerful type of Latin of which Al Capone is the prototype. He had a huge head set upon a bull-like neck, and his physical strength was, weight for weight, proportionate with that of the animal he, in some degree, resembled. The facial lineaments of the signor were, to say the very least of it, not prepossessing. He had a bulbous and broken-nose, a hideous squint of one eye which made it difficult to be certain just in which direction he was looking, thick lips which mostly were open and disclosed what remained of a set of teeth, the majority of which had been knocked out in some affray or other and, left unattended to, were now so many black and broken stumps. Not even the oily suavity of his manner could make up for the unpleasantness of his overdressed and much-bediamonded person. But the dope he trafficked in did all that for him; no addict in the world, starved for their drug, who does not look upon the supplier as some beneficent angel sent by a merciful dispensation of Providence.

Inspector McCarthy knew the signor quite well, almost as well as the signor thought he knew him. There were not many places in his native Soho which McCarthy did not know the ins and outs of, particularly such places as dispensed food and liquor in conjunction with other more or less dubious entertainment. Speaking most Continental languages fluently and being, as he was, an adept at disguise; actually, Signor Raffi knew the Inspector under several names, and had conversed with him at moments when he had not the faintest idea that Inspector McCarthy was within miles of the place. In this way the Inspector had gleaned far more than had ever been learned of Raffi by strictly official methods; quite sufficient to know that there were many angles to the signor's methods of piling up assets—most of them unholy.

Arrived in the vicinity of the *Café di Villarosa*, McCarthy took a good look round for Fox but could see nothing of him, which suggested that Raffi's guest had departed and Fox was sticking to him.

Entering the swing-doors of what constituted the "restaurant" portion of the place, McCarthy found no one there but a few waiters, most of whom had left their joint and several countries to that country's good and, he also knew, were well and truly listed in the Records Room of the Yard. Let any one of them put a foot wrong openly, and it would be Hey Ho! for quick warrants and a deportation-order to finish.

But that all of them knew McCarthy, and just who and what he was very plain to see from the scowls that instantly darkened their countenances at their first glance at him. One, stationed at the upper end of the room nearest that office, was gliding swiftly towards its door when McCarthy, in a soft, almost chiding voice, stopped him.

"No, no, Giuseppe," he said. "You needn't advise the Great and Only Boss that I'm here. I'll do that for myself. *Sapeti?*"

With a muttered: "Si, Signor," that sounded more like a curse than anything else, the man slunk back, and McCarthy, without any attempt at formality, opened the door and walked straight in upon the considerably surprised restaurant-keeper.

"Ah, Raffi!" he hailed amiably, noting the start of surprise Raffi gave when he discovered the identity of his visitor, "surprised to see me at this time of day? *And* a little something else, eh?"

The signor's face promptly became a smiling mask, but that could not prevent beads of perspiration from starting suddenly upon his oily forehead.

"Ah, the Inspector," he exclaimed in tones which he hoped suggested that if there was any one man more than another he was delighted to pay him a surprise visit, that man was Inspector McCarthy. He waved a fat, beringed hand towards a vacant chair and promptly produced a box of Corona-Coronas from his desk.

McCarthy accepted the former, but rejected the latter with a gesture.

"Too early for cigars, Raffi," he said, "and, besides, I'm not over-keen on them, even in the best of circumstances."

"A peety," the signor breathed, and replaced the box.

"I've just dropped in to ask you a question or two," McCarthy went on casually. "Nothing of any great importance in so far as your business here is concerned; just something I want to know."

Signor Raffi shrugged his wide, fat-embedded shoulders.

"Anyt'ing I can tell you, Inspector, it eesa da great pleasure."

"I'm sure it is," McCarthy answered in the same smooth tone. "What I want to know is: Who was the gentleman you had in this office just a little while ago—a gentleman of colour; brown, not black."

For the space of perhaps a split-second a startled, uneasy look came into Raffi's black eyes; in the next it had disappeared, and he was smiling as before.

"There eesa da meestake, Inspector," he said calmly. "Alla da morn' I seet here by myself and go over da books. *Por Bac-cho*—yees."

"That's strange," McCarthy said.

"Howa you mean—strange?" Raffi asked softly. "I tella you I was by myself here and dere was no one else."

"That's the strange part of it," McCarthy informed him. "Someone whose word I can rely upon far more than I can yours, Joseph, informed me very positively that there *was*. And," he added with a snap, "he was right!"

He leaned forward and fixed the Sicilian with a cold, hard stare.

"Now, look here, Raffi," he said, "if you're a wise man, you'll give me the information I'm seeking. I'll get it—anyhow, you can depend on that. But the best thing you can do, in your own interests, is to give it to me and save me a lot of time, and yourself a lot of trouble you won't welcome."

The Sicilian's eyes glinted wickedly for a second, then became perfectly blank.

"I notta know any coloured man," he said stubbornly. "I notta allow them 'ere."

"It's not a customer I'm talking about," McCarthy returned promptly. "You know that as well as I do."

But Raffi allowed no muscle of his fat face to show that the Inspector was right. Instead, he shrugged his huge shoulders again and made a little gesture of bewilderment with his hands.

"You been told wrong, Inspector," he said. "Eef there had been anyone here, likea you say, I tella you at once. Why not? I amma da 'onest man. I gotta not'ing to be afraid of. Da police, or no one else."

A statement this, which very nearly caused McCarthy to laugh outright in the speaker's face.

"We won't go into that just now, Raffi," he said. "For one reason, I haven't the time, and, for another, my 'Sooper' would prefer to handle you personally. He's been itching to do it for quite a long time, and I have the idea that his wish won't be very long delayed. You know who I mean—Superintendent Burman."

The signor knew perfectly well who was being meant, without that person being mentioned by name. Also, he was perfectly well aware of the Superintendent's intentions towards him if ever the chance came his way. If there was one man in London whom the Signor Raffi would have willingly driven a knife into or, at any rate, have had it done by proxy, that man was Superintendent Burman. At the very mention of his name he scowled fiercely.

"I tella you again I notta da know what you talk about," he asseverated savagely.

Again McCarthy leaned forward.

"I'm talking about a brown-skinned man; a heavily-built, powerful fellow with a hook-nose and fearsome black eyes," he recited succinctly. "He's been here with you this morning; not so long gone. He may be a Hindu, though I believe not. He may possibly be an Egyptian, but at any rate he's from one of the Eastern countries. Are you going to tell me who he is, or aren't you?"

The signor shook his head. Any expression that had been in his face before, vanished instantly.

"How you t'ink I tella you somet'ing I notta know myself?" he questioned. "How you tink' I give you da name of someone you say is here when dere ees nobody here."

"I said *was* here, Raffi," McCarthy said grimly. "Not *is!* You're a cunning rat, but you won't get away with twisting words."

"Well, who you *t'ink* it is?" the Sicilian asked with a capital assumption of honest, if bewildered indignation.

McCarthy eyed him coldly. He realised, now, that, whoever this man might prove to be, no threats of his were going to induce Raffi to disclose his identity. Which was sufficient to tell McCarthy that, whatever his nationality, and whatever his connection with Raffi, he must be a big man in one or other of the rackets the Sicilian was up to his ears in. Like most, of his kidney, Raffi would have squealed quickly enough if he could have seen the slightest benefit for himself, in so doing, and that he could not, made it plain to the Inspector that he could see a big and ugly come-back if he opened his mouth. It was useless to waste time there, and there was always one thing to be thankful for—Fox was on the man's tail, and the one who could shake him off would have to be clever indeed.

He got up, picked up his hat, and moved towards the door. At it he turned and, for a long moment, surveyed the Sicilian in silence. His quick, and perhaps not expected turn, allowed him to catch the glance of dark and bloody hatred which the Sicilian had flung after him.

"All right, Raffi," he said quietly. "You're not through with me yet, and neither is the gentleman whose identity you're so anxious to keep covered. You know best why."

A cunning gleam came into the black eyes watching him so closely.

"Who you t'ink he is?" Raffi shot quickly again.

"At the present moment I can't even make a guess," McCarthy answered frankly, "but by this time to-morrow I'll tell you all about him. But, just to take a long hazard," he went on, "I'd say he's one of the big shots who's supplying you with some portion of the dope you peddle in this den."

Raffi started to his feet.

"I notta peddle the dope here," he asseverated with wild gesticulations. "Da police, they try to feex eet on me and they can't. You gotta me set and you t'ink I stand for eet! I tella you I don't. The man who says so tells a lie."

McCarthy moved a step towards him, in his eyes a look which made the burly Sicilian fling up a hand as a guard.

"Shut up!" the Scotland Yard man hissed, "or, by the Sainted Mike, I'll knock that last remark of yours clean down your throat. Good day, Signor Raffi—and look out for trouble. It will have you by the short hair before you know where you are!"

For a considerable time after the departure of his most unwelcome guest, Signor Joseph Raffi sat glowering at the wall before him and muttering bloodthirsty threats. Then he consulted with a notebook he took from an inner pocket and, turning to the telephone, dialled a certain number.

"That was a narrow shave!" he muttered in his native tongue. "He only got away from here in time."

McCarthy, accepting his defeat at the hands of the stubborn restaurant-keeper with his usual philosophy, took another taxi and made his way to the Yard. But, singularly enough, it was not the signor who most filled his mind as he went—it was the very beautiful Miss Sophie Ridley who had looked at him so reproachfully out of those very beautiful violet-blue eyes—and to whose owner, by the way, he had made no explanation of the true purpose of his visit to Fortescue Square.

"A rum show for a lovely little creature like that to be set in the middle of," he mused. "Mummies, and parchments, and withered hands! Not to mention the slashed-faced Egyptian gentleman, and, in all probability, four others of the same kidney. Not the place for a girl like that at all."

He thought a good deal about her during lunch, and by the time he had completed his official report upon the case he had decided that, once this wretched business was settled up, to call around and devote a few evenings to taking her about.

But all thoughts of her disappeared when, at five o'clock, his telephone bell jangled and he lifted his receiver to take a trunk call from Reading, Berkshire. At the other end of the line was the tired but tenacious Detective Fox. "That you, Inspector?" he inquired sharply.

" 'Tis me, myself, Fox," McCarthy answered eagerly. "Got anything?"

"A fairish bit, sir," Fox answered laconically. "From Joe Raffi's place my man went to three other flash West End dives, then lunched at the Berkeley."

"The Berkeley!" McCarthy echoed. "He does himself pretty well."

"From there," Detective Fox went on, taking no notice of the interruption, "he went East to a Chinese 'eats-house' in Limehouse Causeway—Soo Cheongs."

"Ha!" McCarthy emitted.

"He evidently had an appointment there with that old arch-scoundrel, Wan How."

For the second time McCarthy let go an exclamation of undiluted surprise. Wan How, keeper of perhaps half a dozen riverside gaming and opium-dens, belonged to an even lower strata of objectionableness than Joe Raffi. That he was an opium-trafficker there was no doubt, but, like the Soho-Sicilian, his cunning had, so far, been too much for the police.

"He stayed with Wan How perhaps half an hour," Fox proceeded, "and, from a corner of the room, I saw Wan How pay him a big packet of Bank of England notes. He kept his taxi running outside and, after the interview, it took him back to Paddington."

"Paddington again!" McCarthy exclaimed excitedly. "Well?"

"He booked to—"

The smashing of a heavy pane of glass smote with startling suddenness upon McCarthy's eardrums. It was followed by a deep groan, then the voice of Fox, gone suddenly faint to a stricken whisper, came over the wire.

"Got me!" he wheezed. "Shot from—"

Then came the thud of a falling body, then—silence.

"Fox!" McCarthy called sharply, but there was no response; Detective Fox had followed his last trail!

CHAPTER X

NO EVIDENCE!

RECEIVER still in hand, McCarthy sat staring at the instrument for a moment of paralysed inaction. Then a voice came through to him; the startled voice of a girl operator.

"Is anything wrong?" she asked. "I thought I heard—"

"You did," McCarthy snapped. "You heard a man shot; a C.I.D. man calling me, Detective Inspector McCarthy, at Scotland Yard. Trace where the call came from and notify your local police to get there on the jump. That clear?"

"Quite," she answered.

"Good," McCarthy said. "I'll hang on. Get me something through as quickly as you can, there's a good lass."

In less than two minutes the girl was speaking to him again.

"The police are on their way there, Inspector," she informed him.

"Good girl, but where?"

"'To a telephone-box in the Caversham Road."

"Caversham!" The word came from McCarthy's lips like the crack of a whip. That was the S-H-A-M of that fragment of post-mark. Poor Grey had indeed been close to someone; someone who had no hesitation in killing whoever or whatever might threaten him. Fox, despite his natural gift of shadowing, had been detected and wiped out ruthlessly at the very moment of his success. But the killer had, in the first place, made the usual mistake that such as he invariably do; the mistake that would hang him at the finish. He had left that one tiny scrap of paper in Grey's pocket and that would, before long, prove to be the beginning of his morning walk to the gallows.

He suddenly realised that he was still standing there with the receiver to his ear.

"Thank you, Miss," he said quietly. "You acted very promptly."

Ringing her off, McCarthy got on to "Phones," downstairs.

"There's been an—an accident at Reading," he said briefly. "Detective Fox is hurt, possibly fatal. Ring the Reading police and get them to send their report through at the earliest possible moment. I'll be upstairs in the Assistant-Commissioner's room for some time; you can get me there."

Making his way upstairs, he completely staggered Sir William Haynes with his grim news.

"Good God, Mac!" the A.C. exclaimed in horror-stricken tones. "This is as terrible as poor Grey's death."

"And brought about by the same hand," McCarthy said. "You can be quite sure of that."

"There's only one hope," Haynes said. "The shot may not have been fatal."

McCarthy shook his head dolefully.

"I'm afraid there's not much chance of that," he returned, "though I'm hoping against hope that we'll hear at any moment that it is that way. But a man who kills as this one does would make certain he'd finished his job. And there's another thing, Bill, which doesn't tend towards the hopeful side. Poor Fox was on the very verge of telling me where he had booked to when he was shot down. But for that telephone girl joining in, it might have been hours before we'd found out just where Fox was killed, and to be shot as he was at the exact moment that he was, seems to say that the killer must have been close on him, quite possibly sufficiently near to have made out what he was saying."

"He could scarcely hear him in a telephone booth, Mac," Haynes reminded him.

"He could probably make out his words by a species of lip-reading—follow Fox's formation of his words. It's been done. When he got to that point he probably came to the conclusion that Fox was passing over dangerous information and it was time to cut him short. He did it with the same callousness as he showed in the Grey murder. Those are the reasons why I don't think there's a hope that Fox is still living. The man must have been close on him for one thing, and Fox was a dangerous man to him for another. I don't expect any good news."

"We can but hope—" the Assistant-Commissioner was beginning, when the telephone-bell cut him off. Lifting the receiver, he listened for a minute. Then:

"Reading," he said briefly.

McCarthy stood waiting anxiously, endeavouring to read from his friend's face and by his curt returns into the instrument just what the news was. But, inwardly, he knew already; the grim set of Haynes' face told him that the worst had happened—Fox was dead.

From the Assistant-Commissioner's returns into the 'phone he made out that the Reading police had picked up nothing whatever as to the actual happening, or the identity of the murderer. That it had been a quick kill, and a still quicker getaway, there seemed to be no doubt.

"Thank you, Superintendent," Haynes said at length. "I'm greatly obliged to you. As this death touches very closely upon a case being handled by Detective-Inspector McCarthy, he will probably be down there at the earliest possible moment to confer with you. No, I don't think that there can be any possible gain in leaving the body where it is. I'd have it removed to the mortuary and the post-mortem conducted as soon as possible. The bullet may tell us something. Thank you. Good day."

"So it is a kill, and they've got nothing," McCarthy said, gloomily.

Haynes nodded sadly.

"Shot stone dead with a heavy-calibre weapon from a passing car. The street seemed to be pretty empty at the time, and as a silenced gun was used, nobody seemed to know what had happened until poor Fox's body was noticed slumped up in the telephone-booth. By which time, of course, the car had got well away and, naturally enough, no one had taken the slightest notice of it as far as number, colour, or anything else."

"And, of course, there's not even the remotest idea as to the identity of the actual killer?"

"How could there be? It was a closed car and, as I tell you, no one seemed to take the slightest notice of it."

"By the Sainted Mike, but I'll have it out of Joe Raffi or that unhung scoundrel, Wan How, before I'm much older, if I pull the pair to pieces," McCarthy declared heatedly.

Haynes shook his head.

"I'm afraid not, Mac," he said. "If Raffi wouldn't speak this morning, he certainly won't now, with a second murder committed—that's if he knows anything about it, of course. As for Wan How, that old ruffian will simply beam at you innocently and 'No savvee' you till you want to hit him. He'll know nothing, have seen nothing, have heard nothing, and simply point out, if you put it to him, that whoever said they saw him with this man was mistaken, and with Fox wiped out you wouldn't have the slightest shred of proof that he was lying."

"By the Lord Harry," McCarthy almost hissed at his superior, "it's cases like this that almost make me believe that the Americans have the right of it with their 'third degree.' They'd have this pair inside and give them something they'd never forget, the longest day of their lives. They'd leave them a pair of wrecks if they survived what they'd get at all. But they'd *talk*. We're as helpless as a pack of kittens. We know damned well that both Raffi or Wan How can give us the name of this man, yet all we're allowed to do is to hand them polite questions. 'Would you be kind enough to tell us this, Mr. Raffi?' Or: 'You'd oblige us greatly if you'd tell us that, Mr. Wan How,' and all the time they're doing just as you say. In the one case: 'No savveeing' us till the cows come home or, in the other, simply standing on the ground that our information's not correct and laughing like hell at us all the time."

Haynes shrugged his shoulders.

"It does seem imbecile, Mac," he said, "but that's the way of it, and the game has got to be played by the rules."

McCarthy moodily stumped up and down the room for a moment, then suddenly came to a full stop with an exclamation which made Haynes stare at his companion.

"Well, of all the blithering idiots!" he began. "Of all the complete and utter mental shortages on earth at this moment, I'm the champion."

"What's got you?" the A.C. asked in surprise.

"There's one man who can tell me exactly who this merchant is; a man of totally different character—Professor Farman. Don't forget, as I did, that he was the first man to be with him this morning! He's bound to know the man's identity."

"Not necessarily," Haynes said. "He probably will know just what he's been told by the man himself, concerning his identity. If, as I'm beginning to think, the man happens to be an Egyptian, that fact alone would more than likely interest a man whose sole hobby is Egyptology. But it doesn't say that he really knows anything about the fellow."

McCarthy rubbed his clean-shaven chin thoughtfully.

"You mean that he may probably be only a Museum acquaintance, and that the Professor's meeting with him this morning, when Fox saw them, was nothing but the merest coincidence?"

"I'm not saying that it is so," Haynes said, "I'm merely pointing out the possibility, if not the probability, that it *may* be so. After all, the Farmans of this world don't consort with double-dyed murderers."

"They don't *knowingly*, Bill," the Inspector agreed, "but you can bet that this gentleman is as suave as they make them. Nobody's going to know what he is from either his externals or his manner. However, I've an idea that I'll make his acquaintance before I'm so much older, and if I put the man who killed both Grey and Fox in the dock, I don't care a damn if I never do another job as long as I live."

CHAPTER XI

IN WHICH INSPECTOR McCARTHY STILL BUTTS THE IMPENETRABLE STONE WALL

IT was as McCarthy made his way towards Fortescue Square that another thought crossed his mind which took him hurriedly to the nearest 'phone and into touch again with Sir William Haynes.

"Bill," he said, "with the shock of this murder there's one thing I've completely forgotten."

"What's that?" Haynes asked.

"Why, that I took Fox off the job of guarding the professor and sent him after this Egyptian. As it stands, there's no one looking after Farman now. Put a good man on to the job right away, will you? Let him start watching the house—he'll be bound to pick him up sooner or later. Once he does, have him keep contact with you as often as is possible. Get him on the job right away."

"I'll send a man to Fortescue Square at once," Haynes said.

Arrived in the square, McCarthy took stock of the house from a distance. He had no particular wish to fall under the watchful eyes of Mr. Ali if he could possibly avoid it. What he had to say was for the professor's ear alone—there was still in his mind the very strong possibility that this evil-looking five might be mixed up with the murderer of Grey and Fox. But, carefully as he surveyed the place, he could see no sign of the Egyptian; for the matter of that, there was no sign of life visible about the house at all.

A glance at that upper window showed it, too, to be empty—as a matter of fact its blinds were drawn. Somehow it struck McCarthy that the house looked more cheerless than ever; for a reason which he could not have defined for a moment, it seemed to have taken on a sinister aspect since he had seen it last. Which, on the face of it, seemed utterly ridiculous.

"That's the curse of me Irish ancestry," he apostrophised himself. "I've got more imagination than brains, and I don't suppose the Italian half of me does much to counteract it."

The hunch struck him to take a look at the back of the premises, but there the same conditions prevailed, only more so, for all the blinds at the back of the house were drawn.

"Which almost looks as though they'd suddenly gone away," he commented musingly.

Returning to the front, he went up the steps and pressed heavily upon the bell-push. Upon his last visit he had very distinctly heard the sound of the bell in the hall; so much so that he had noted its deep and rather booming note. But, this time, there came no sound at all.

"Queer," he exclaimed puzzledly. "Can't have been cut off, surely. Must have gone wrong."

Lifting the heavy, old-fashioned knocker with which the door was furnished, he knocked loudly upon it but still there was no answer. Several times he repeated it, until forced to the conclusion that the house was empty. He decided to make a further test of it by returning to the telephone-booth and ringing the house.

But that plan, when put into execution, proved to be just as ineffectual as the rest. Getting into communication with anyone in Professor Farman's house seemed to be an utter impossibility. He wondered what Miss Sophie Ridley was up to that she, at any rate, had not heard the din he had kicked up. As far as he had been able to gather from her, she never left the house except for her evening walks. Unless, of course, the professor had had some sudden call away connected with his researches and had needed her with him. That was always possible. He would give the place another try later, but first he must make for Reading and see what he could pick up concerning the murder of Fox.

But upon arrival there he found that everything that could possibly have been done had been handled by the Berkshire constabulary with the greatest thoroughness. But, out of it, there had come exactly nil. Owing to the fact that Fox had been shot from a passing car, there was nothing whatever in the way of fingerprints or spoor of feet to search for, and as for a trace as to whose the car had been, or even a description of it, there was not the slightest sign of a clue.

As McCarthy already knew, Fox must have been killed by a "silenced" weapon, or he, himself, *must* have heard the report of a heavy-calibred gun simultaneously with the crashing of the glass. That accounted for the fact that no one of the few who had chanced to be in the street at the moment took the slightest notice of the car, but gave all their attention to the telephone-box, by which time the vehicle had disappeared completely, leaving no trace whatever of the direction it had taken. As far as the car or its occupants were concerned, McCarthy was up against a blank wall.

He made no special mention of the fragment of partially-stamped envelope he had found in Grey's pocket, but proceeded to make a few quite casual-sounding inquiries as to the Caversham district and its residents.

He found that it lay upon the other side of the river and consisted, in the main, of large houses situated for the greater part upon the Heights and occupied by well-to-do-people. It was a part only approachable on foot, or by private car, which most, if not all, of the residents possessed. In nine cases out of every ten they were well known London business people with a leaven of independent persons and gentlemen of the learned processions.

The local Superintendent eyed him curiously.

"Why do you ask, Inspector?" he inquired. "Surely not with the idea that any Caversham resident could have anything to do with this case?"

"Good Lord, no," McCarthy assured him. "It's just that there's something of interest to me about the place, and I thought you'd be the man who could tell me as much about it as the next."

"I can tell you all there is to know about it," the "Sooper" told him. "I go all over that part at least every week, and those of the residents I don't know personally, I have a pretty good idea of their general status and I can tell you that they're quite all right."

"Thanks," McCarthy said laconically and, in the same casual manner inquired from the officer if among them he knew there was anyone answering to the description of the man who had met Professor Farman that morning residing in that locality. That the Superintendent knew of, there was not.

"Unless," he added, "it's someone who's come there very recently."

As McCarthy had no knowledge upon this point, he followed it no further—for the present at any rate. Until some trace could be found of the murder-weapon the killer could sit and laugh at them. Arranging for the remains of the unfortunate Fox to be conveyed to London—McCarthy thanked his stars that he had not been a married man, or the job of breaking the news to his wife would have most assuredly have fallen upon his shoulders—he accepted the offer of a lift back to Town in one of the Berkshire police cars. He was not finished with Caversham—not by a very long way. He proposed to put that well-to-do locality through the sieve in his own time and in his own way, which meant without the aid of the Berkshire Constabulary, efficient though they were.

On the way back he did some extremely hard thinking, answering in monosyllables the attempts at polite conversation put forward by his driver. One thing was weighing considerably on his mind: the closed up and silent house in Fortescue Square. He determined upon paying it another visit. If it was still in the same condition then there would most certainly be a Yard man somewhere in the vicinity.

In next to no time he found him and, with a beckoning nod for him to follow, strolled around the nearest corner.

"Have you seen anything of Professor Farman to-day?" he asked, quite expecting to be answered in the negative.

But it seemed that about two hours before the professor had left the house and gone as far as the British Museum where, for some hour and three quarters or so, he had read in the Egyptian section, then returned to the house. That was the only time that the shadow had set eyes on him that day.

"Thank heaven he's all right up to now," McCarthy said with a sigh of relief. "Keep a tight eye upon him, Jenkins, and be ready to jump in at the slightest thing that seems to you suspicious-looking."

Leaving the man, McCarthy went up to the front door and rang, to be instantly opened to by the smouldering-eyed Ali. This time he very plainly heard the bell, which, obviously, had been put in order since his previous visit. In answer to his query as to whether Professor Farman were at home, Ali, with a gesture, motioned him to enter, then went and called the professor from that room in which McCarthy had examined the body of Grey.

The professor's greeting was most cordial, and he instantly invited the Inspector into the room and closed the door.

"What can I do for you this time, Inspector?" he asked, then, before McCarthy could answer, went on. "You'll quite understand, I hope, my reason for declining the bodyguard you so kindly suggested for me? Apart from any other consideration, the fact that I do a lot of my research in places to which any such person would not be admitted carried great weight with me, and nothing, not even danger, must interfere with my studies. They come before everything. I trust you understand?"

"Perfectly; perfectly," McCarthy assured him heartily and keeping entirely to himself the fact that the professor was being quite as well tailed as any man in London was likely to be.

"I've come to ask a question, sir, that you possibly may think impertinent but, I can assure you, I do not ask it without the very best of reasons."

Professor Farman looked at him queerly for a moment, then frowned puzzledly.

"Why should it be impertinent, Inspector, since there is proper reason for asking it?"

"I want to learn, if you can possibly tell me, the identity of the man with whom you spoke in the Egyptian section of the British Museum this morning."

A hard glint sprang suddenly into the professor's eyes.

"Peppery man, if rubbed the wrong way," McCarthy thought to himself.

"Am I to understand by that question," the professor broke out heatedly, "that my movements are being watched? That I am under surveillance? By Heaven, sir, but this is an outrage after my distinctly-expressed refusal to have anyone tacked on to me. I shall communicate with the Commissioner of Police immediately."

"Now, sir," McCarthy began cajolingly, "you have entirely the wrong idea of it. Nothing was further from the minds of anyone than that your actions should be watched in any way. If you're under the impression that we've placed a guard over you, you're entirely mistaken," he lied fluently. "It happened by the merest coincidence that one of the Special-Branch men happened to be in that section."

"An obvious fabrication!" the professor snorted. "What would a policeman be doing there?"

"Precisely the same thing that poor Grey was," McCarthy answered quietly, thanking Heaven for the aptness of his answer.

"You mean," the professor asked, "that he, too, was interested in Egyptian opium?"

"Exactly," McCarthy said, "and he happened to notice, quite casually, that a certain man in whom he was interested holding a conversation with yourself."

"A man in whom Scotland Yard is interested holding a conversation with me?" the professor echoed, incredulously.

"Just so," McCarthy said; "I would be very glad if you could give me any clue as to his identity."

"But I spoke with half a dozen or more men in the course of the morning," Professor Farman answered. "That is a common enough occurrence. If I may say so," he went on, "I am accepted as one of the greatest living authorities in Egyptian research, and many people do me the honour of inquiring my views upon the subject. It is my invariable custom to give them such information as is in my power."

"This particular man either gave, or exchanged some papers with you," McCarthy persisted.

The professor shrugged his shoulders.

"Another thing equally as common as accosting me," he returned. From his pocket he pulled quite a little packet of papers covered with different handwritings, upon many of which were what McCarthy knew to be roughly drawn Egyptian hieroglyphics.

"All of these have been passed to me either in the form of inquiry, or theory, within the last morning or two. You will see, Inspector, how difficult it is for me to pick out any particular person you may have in mind."

"This man," McCarthy went on, "was heavy in build and of the colour and type of countenance which might easily be set down as Egyptian."

The professor frowned thoughtfully for a moment, then looked through the little sheaf of papers.

"I believe I *do* know the man you mean," he said, "and, if I am correct, he is an Egyptian, as you surmised. He was greatly interested in some excavation work which he had seen begun at Thebes some years ago. He, himself, is not unversed in the ancient hieroglyphics, he informed me, and showed me, or perhaps I should say, gave me a copy of some attempts of his to translate the ancient symbols into the English language. I have his attempts here," the professor said, handing out two of the papers McCarthy had noted. "Not very happy ones, I'm afraid, though it's possible that if he perseveres he may do considerably better."

"His name, Professor?" McCarthy asked eagerly. "No doubt he gave you that?"

"As it happens," Farman answered, "he did not, nor did I ask it. The only possible thing of interest between us was Egyptology—his name was a matter of complete indifference to me."

Stifling a groan of disappointment, McCarthy asked if, by any chance, he had mentioned his place of residence, to be told, almost contemptuously, that that had even less interest for the man of research than his name.

"Even had he mentioned it, which he did not," the professor said, "it would have undoubtedly have gone completely from my memory which, in such matters, is perfectly hopeless. In such things I have to rely almost entirely upon Miss Ridley."

"Then you can give me no assistance whatever," McCarthy said, a sense of disappointment heavy upon him.

"Not the slightest, I'm afraid," Farman said. "But, should this man speak to me again in the Museum I will certainly do my best to acquire the information you want."

Which was not over-hopeful, but left one possible loophole.

"Do I understand, sir?" McCarthy asked, "that the man referred to was a regular frequenter of that portion of the Museum?"

Professor Farman thought for a moment.

"I would not say that," he answered, "but I have certainly seen him there upon several occasions."

McCarthy got up and picked up his hat.

"Thank you, sir," he said. "I don't think I need waste your time any further. I'm sorry not to have been able to get the identity of the man, but I dare say we'll pick it up in some other direction before long."

"And just what, if I may ask, is the police interest in this particular student of Egyptology?" the professor inquired.

McCarthy smiled, and shook his head.

"That, I'm afraid, must come under the heading of 'Official Secrets,' sir," he replied. "At any rate for the present."

Then he took his departure.

CHAPTER XII

THE INSPECTOR DECIDES UPON A VISIT TO THE EAST

IT was as McCarthy made his way along to the taxi-rank by the corner that the thought occurred to him that, in keeping everything he knew to himself, he might quite possibly have done the professor a considerable disservice.

Whether or not it would not have been better policy to have given the professor the warning that the man he was inquiring for was the one he believed to be guilty of the murder of Grey and, therefore, if the prophecy of the withered hand was to be taken into any consideration, a menace to himself, was an open question.

On the other hand, although the professor seemed to have recovered his shaken nerve in truly remarkable manner, whether the knowledge might not stampede him into some foolish act had also to be considered. Or, if not that, its effect might be, from sheer motives of self-preservation, realising how close they could get to him outside, to have him shut himself up in the house, a complete recluse until the immediate danger had passed.

He found himself wondering where Miss Ridley had been, not only during the interview just finished, but also at the time of his earlier visit, when the house had seemed to be completely deserted. It would, in a sense, have been a relief to have caught sight of her, if only as an assurance that she was perfectly all right. Though, he was bound to admit, it seemed foolish to consider the possibility of her being anything else in a house such as that of Professor Farman. After all, even mummies, unpleasant-looking Egyptian servants and other kindred things, gruesome as they might be as a surrounding, did not constitute any actual menace.

Well, the possibility of the professor being able to supply the identity of the mysterious Oriental having entirely departed, he would have to search for an identifier in other directions. Of two known to have had dealings with the man, there remained Wan How and Joe Raffi. That the latter would have altered, or could be cajoled or threatened into altering his former stubborn attitude was unlikely; McCarthy knew the Sicilian well enough to be aware that to break Raffi's obduracy he would have to have recourse to the very strongest methods permitted him.

Had he been able to have applied for a warrant charging Raffi with either complicity in, or being an accessory before or after the fact in the murders of either Grey or Fox, he would have had that unholy scoundrel "squealing" in no time. But he was only too well aware that, despite the unhallowed joy it would have given the authorities to have laid Raffi by the heels on a serious charge, he would never be granted a warrant upon such slim evidence as he could offer.

Looking at it calmly, he could see that perfectly clearly. All that he had to put forward in his request was the telephoned word of a police officer, since dead, that this unknown man had visited Raffi and had been closeted with him in his back office. This Raffi denied, and would go on denying until he was really scared for his own safety, and there was not one real tittle of evidence to say that he was lying. No; as far as matters had progressed, there was little hope of forcing Raffi to speak by those means.

Wan How?

The position with regard to that wily old scoundrel was exactly the same. Fox had reported that the mystery Oriental had gone down to Soo Cheong's Limehouse dive and there had what had evidently been a pre-arranged interview with the big Yellow Boss of the riverfront. He, moreover, reported that the old Chinaman had passed over a large sum of money in notes to the other. What for, if not a deal of some kind, and what deal could there possibly be in which Wan How would be interested, except one of two things—dope, in some sort or other, though almost of a certainty opium, or women for his riverside dens.

But could Wan How be made to talk? McCarthy knew perfectly well that the subtle-minded old Celestial would stall him off with just as much effect as the pig-headed stubborn equivocation of Joe Raffi, and that there was just as much hope of getting any information out of the yellows, or half-castes, or even whites, for the matter of that, who used Soo Cheong's as a hang-out, as there was of inducing one of Raffi's Sicilian waiters to talk about their boss. If that was the angle which would have to be worked, it would mean a personal visit to Soo Cheong's in some disguise or other, and a stay in that notorious den until he could pick up something for himself. And that was the very last thing he wanted to be forced to do at the moment.

Arrived back at the Yard, he had a further session with the Assistant-Commissioner.

"My idea that Professor Farman might give me the identity of this man has flopped hopelessly, Bill," he reported. "He's a complete stranger to him, though he says he's seen him more than once at that department at the Museum. It appears that the man's also a bit of an amateur on Egyptology, and the papers which were seen to pass between himself and Professor Farman were just some notes on Egyptian hieroglyphics. I saw them myself," he went on gloomily, "and they looked like something a fly might have done with its hind legs after it had crawled out of an inkpot."

"Terrible things, hieroglyphics, to people who aren't versed in them," Haynes said. "Well, what's your next move, Mac?"

McCarthy shook his head:

"At the present moment," he answered, "it looks as if I'll have to do a spell down in the docklands and see what I can worm out of Soo Cheong, or some one or other of the gang that infest his place."

"That means time, Mac," the Assistant-Commissioner said.

"Don't I know it," McCarthy said with a sigh, "to say nothing of the job of finding out anything that Wan How is doing. The mere mention of that old devil's name sends them stone deaf in both ears and dumber than any oyster. His hatchet-men have put the fear of God properly into all the river toughs."

"But why Soo Cheong's?" Haynes asked. "Why not Wan How's, itself?"

"Because it was at Soo Cheong's that they met, and obviously by appointment," McCarthy pointed out.

"But that only proves the cunning of the old swine," Haynes objected. "He simply would not have any traces of this man having come to his place. Particularly would he avoid that if he had any knowledge of, or part in, the murder in Fortescue Square the night before. It's just up to the cunning old rat to drag someone else into it, and it would suit his book to see Soo Cheong land into trouble."

"If all I can hear is true," McCarthy said dubiously, "Wan How is Soo Cheong's boss, and the place is just as much his as the other dives we know he runs."

"Which probably means that, for reasons of his own, he wouldn't mind landing Soo Cheong in trouble. Worked discreetly, it might give him a good excuse with the Tongs for having Soo Cheong wiped out. You never can tell with a cunning old rat like that—he'd soon think up some cock and bull story that Soo Cheong had played him false, and the Tong hatchet-men would soon see that he joined the spirits of his ancestry. The Tong men themselves aren't very brainy, though, Heaven knows, their leaders are. No,

Mac, if you'll take my earnest advice, you'll start the ball rolling at Wan How's and waste no time with Soo Cheong."

"Perhaps you're right," McCarthy said. "Lord knows there's no time to be lost, and I don't want to waste even an hour on a false trail. But I'll tell you one thing, Bill," he added. "It's going to take me a bit of thinking to get me into Wan How's No. 1 place. The last time I paid him a protracted visit brought such a heap of trouble upon the old devil, not to mention about five hundred pounds in fines, that he's sworn to have me rubbed out on sight. He won't be in it, that goes without saying, but he'll see that it's done, nevertheless."

The Assistant-Commissioner thought frowningly for a moment.

"Let's see," he said. "It's quite a time since Limehouse renewed its acquaintance with that delightful Italian sailor-man, the Signor Pietro Sperozza, if I remember rightly," he observed, a twinkle in his eyes.

McCarthy grinned:

"It is," he agreed. "Two years or more. And I'm bound to admit that the stink the signor kicked up upon his last appearance there has scarcely died down yet."

"You've no reason for believing that Wan How, or any of the Chinese colony have the slightest inkling as to the true identity of Pietro Sperozza?"

"I'd bet on that," McCarthy said with certainty. "That is," he amended hastily, "with one exception."

"Who is that?" Haynes asked.

"My very good old friend, Doctor Quong See. The old man was caught in an ugly jam one night with some hooligans who meant robbing him, and I was obliged to let my identity be disclosed to get him out of it. That wasn't in the East End, though, and I'll lay my life that old Quong See would never utter a syllable of what he learned to anyone, yellow or white. In a sort of a way, I saved his life—the gang who were at him wouldn't have stopped at much to have got what he was carrying on him. As he told me after, I'd earned his undying gratitude, and a day would come, and all that sort of thing."

"Doctor Quong See," Haynes mused, "as great an influence for good in Chinatown as Wan How is for bad."

"And the two hate each other like the very divil," McCarthy said. "No, Quong See certainly wouldn't tell the man who is, perhaps, his bitterest enemy, who Pietro Sperozza is."

He got up and paced the room a moment.

"But, mind you, Bill," he continued, "I'm not for a moment underestimating either the cunning of Wan How or his organisation for information. What that old devil doesn't know about who goes into, or who goes out of Chinatown doesn't matter. But I'm pretty sure he isn't aware of that. But, all the same, I'll slip down to Chinatown to-night and prepare a first-class alibi which, I hope, may disarm any suspicions Wan How may have—or anyone else."

"How do you propose doing that?" Haynes asked.

"Leave that to me," McCarthy said, and turned to the door as Haynes' 'phone rang out sharply.

CHAPTER XIII

IN WHICH McCARTHY LEARNS OF THE EXISTENCE OF A CERTAIN MR. JUNG DORASSO

ALMOST subconsciously, and without the slightest intention of listening-in upon his friend's conversation, McCarthy paused while Haynes lifted the receiver. A moment he listened, then pushed the instrument towards the inspector.

"For you," he said. " 'Phones' been trying to get you in your room and failed, then tried here on the offchance."

"Hullo?" McCarthy asked, wondering who was likely to be on the line to him at that particular hour, and deciding on the instant that it must be the man he had left on duty at Fortescue Square. But, to his utter and complete surprise, his caller was no other than Miss Sophie Ridley.

"Inspector McCarthy speaking?" she asked.

"The same, Miss Ridley," he answered quickly. "This is a great surprise. A very pleasant one, of course, but a surprise, for all that. You are ringing from Fortescue Square?"

"No," she answered. "From a telephone-booth in Russell Square station."

A strained note in her voice told him instantly that she was labouring under a certain amount of agitation.

"Is anything the matter?" he asked quickly.

"Well, yes—and no," she answered. "I wanted to ask you to do me a very great favour."

"Anything I possibly can do, Miss Ridley, consider it done," McCarthy assured her earnestly.

"I wanted to ask you," she went on, "not to come to the house again, or, if you must do so, to kindly both make no mention of, or take not the slightest notice of myself, should I happen to be about."

"Whatever has happened for you to ask that?" McCarthy questioned.

"Simply that I got into the most frightful trouble when Professor Farman got back and I told him of your visit and our conversation. He went almost livid with rage and told me that I had no right to exchange even two words with you. He was so unlike his usual self that he frightened me, and, I am afraid, I am still scared. It was terrible while it lasted."

"I'm most frightfully sorry," McCarthy said quietly, and wondering as he spoke just what was at the bottom of the professor's anger. That he could be hot-tempered enough when put out, he was well aware; his manner when he jumped to the rightful conclusion that he had been 'tailed' showed that instantly. But why be upset about a call from himself, the officer whom he knew to be in charge of an ugly murder committed upon his own threshold. And, anyhow, why vent it upon the girl?

"I really can't see why the professor should raise objections, at any rate in that manner," he continued. "Our conversation was harmless enough, surely."

It occurred to him as queer that the professor had not made any mention of all this when he had seen him. He came to the conclusion that, like a good many more, he could vent his spleen freely enough upon someone who was powerless to protect themselves, but he would give considerable thought to an open quarrel with someone who could not only look well after himself, but could put the professor in his place without the slightest trouble and, additionally, be backed by authority in the act. He was disappointed in the professor.

"What happened?" he asked tersely.

"He made me repeat our conversation over and over again until I was sure that I had every word of it pat," she told him, "then he evidently came to the conclusion that he had been making a great to do about nothing, for he apologised to me for what he called 'the abruptness of his tone.' But it was far more than that, I can assure you. Then he and Ali and two of the other men went into the Museum—I mean his private museum, of course," she said, "and there they've been working ever since, at any rate until the professor went out this afternoon."

"Do you mean to say that the professor and his men have been in the house until he went out this afternoon?" he inquired sharply.

"Yes," she told him again.

"And you, yourself?" McCarthy questioned keenly. "You have been there the greater part of, if not all the day?"

"Yes," she told him again.

"Then can you tell me how it was that when I called this morning I could get no answer to my persistent knocking, and the blinds were for the greater part drawn and the house seemed to be deserted?"

"Was that you?" she exclaimed in a tone of unfeigned surprise. "I heard the knocking and wondered why they did not answer it. I came to the conclusion that it must be either that they could not hear it in the museum, or that the professor absolutely refused to be disturbed in his work by anyone. Really I think it must be the former, for I was kicking up a fearful din myself and they certainly did not hear me. Ali was most apologetic about it afterwards."

"About what, Miss Ridley?" McCarthy asked.

"Well, after this 'scene,' if you could call it that, with the professor, I went into the small study to do some copying. As a matter of fact, Inspector," she admitted in a voice which still had a quaver in it, "I went there to have a good cry as much as anything, and, somehow or other, I must have jammed the lock of the door and I could not get out again. The key was upon the outside, and although I was only two or three doors from the museum and banged and banged with a book, they could not hear me. Both Ali and the professor assured me of that, therefore I suppose they could not hear you."

"Seems feasible enough," McCarthy said. "They must be most frightfully engrossed in whatever they do there," he remarked tentatively.

"They work upon the mummies, of course," she informed him. "I can always tell when they're at that because of the dreadful sickly smell which pervades the whole house."

"Smell?" McCarthy questioned.

"It is always there when the mummy-cases are opened," she said. "The professor once told me when I asked that it came from the hundreds of yards of swathings that the bodies are wrapped in, and the unguents used to embalm them."

"Sounds cheerful," McCarthy returned. "I'm afraid that the place and its gruesome surroundings are getting on your nerves, Miss Ridley. I'm not so sure that a little of it wouldn't get on mine, either."

He heard her nervous little laugh before she answered.

"I'm afraid you're right," she said. "Ever since the professor stormed at me I've had a horribly frightened feeling. It's made me think things that never entered my mind before and ever since the row I've had a feeling that Ali is watching me. I suppose it all sounds too utterly ridiculous to you, but I've got an awful feeling that there's something uncanny about the place. I know it must sound extremely foolish to you, but I can't shake it off."

McCarthy thought for a moment.

"It doesn't sound foolish to me, at all Miss Ridley," he said quietly. "It seems perfectly natural that that sort of thing should attack you, surrounded by those horrible things and, to put it plainly, not particularly pleasant people. What makes you think that this man Ali is watching you?"

"That, too, may be purely a fancy of mine," she answered, "but ever since they got that jammed door open I've caught him—or thought I did—looking at me in the strangest way. Once or twice I've got right out of his sight, but, for one reason or another, he very soon has me in it again. The professor I have not seen since. I knew that he'd gone to the Museum because I'd prepared some papers for him and they were gone, and I knew that nobody else would have touched them, nor would he, except for that purpose."

"And yet they made no objection to your going out this evening?" McCarthy put.

"Not the slightest," she said. "I just put on my hat and coat as I always do and, although Ali was in the hall, he made no effort to stop me or suggest my not going."

"Then how do you know you're not being watched now?"

He heard her startled exclamation over the line.

"I—I don't know! I never even gave it a thought. All I wanted to do was get out of the house and make sure that you did not, quite inadvertently, bring more trouble upon me."

"You can rest assured I shall not do that," McCarthy told her. "Look here, Miss Ridley. One frank question. Are you really frightened? Have you really got it set in your mind that any harm might come to you from anyone in that house?"

"I—I don't know," she answered falteringly. "If you'd asked me that yesterday I should have answered without the slightest hesitation that I was not, but to-day—"

"To-day you're not so certain," McCarthy completed for her. "Now, look here, Miss Ridley, take down this number I give you and if ever the slightest thing occurs in that house to frighten you again, just get to the telephone and dial that number and call help. It's the nearest police-station to you and I'll take particular care that within an hour they'll be instructed just what to do. They'll trace the call and be in Fortescue Square on the run."

"I may be dead by then," she said, and he could almost see the wan little smile with which she spoke the words.

"Any more of that, young lady," he said sternly, "and you'll get a good talking-to. And, anyhow," he added whimsically, "even if you are they'll make them produce the body, and that won't please them any too much. Anything else?"

"No; good-bye."

"*Au 'voir*," McCarthy corrected, and, as he was about to replace the receiver, a sudden thought flashed across his mind.

"One moment," he well-nigh shouted into the 'phone. "I think you told me that the professor had a few callers who are permitted into his museum and private places generally."

"Very, very few," she said.

"True. But some," McCarthy persisted. "Does any one of them resemble this description?"

With as much detail as he could, he limned a verbal portrait of the man who had hurried out of the square; the man whom Fox had followed until death, swift and sudden, overtook him.

"Why, yes," she said the moment he had finished. "That is an exact picture of Mr. Jung Dorasso."

"Ha!" McCarthy emitted. "And he, perhaps, is a very great friend of the professor and calls often?"

"Very often," she said simply, "and, as an actual matter of fact, I believe is the only one who is allowed into the museum."

"Ah," McCarthy breathed on a long-drawn inbreath. "And what type of man is this Mr. Jung Dorasso?"

"A horrible, smirking beast!" she cried vehemently. "I detest him! The moment he comes into the house I go straight to my own rooms. I did last night."

"Last night!" McCarthy exclaimed. "Are you telling me that this man was in Professor Farman's house last night?"

"He was there just before Mr. Grey," she told him. "As a matter of fact, as the door must have closed upon Mr. Grey I really thought it was Dorasso going."

A low whistle came from McCarthy.

"I see," he said slowly. "And where does this Mr. Dorasso live, do you happen to know?"

"That I cannot tell you. I have never heard it mentioned. Good-bye. You will be very careful not to say anything of this talk to the professor?"

Having assured her upon this point, McCarthy rang off, and stood in silent, frowning thought for a minute or two. "So the professor did know this mysterious Mr. Jung Dorasso, after all?" he said to himself, but aloud.

"And who may Mr. Jung Dorasso be, when he's at home?" Haynes asked.

"That remains to be found out," McCarthy answered evasively, "and the point isn't quite so much *who* he is when he's at home, but *where* is he when he's at that same place?"

He moved again to the door.

"What is your move to be, Mac?" the Assistant-Commissioner asked.

McCarthy shrugged his shoulders.

"I'm contemplating two distinct moves, Bill," he answered, "and that's all I care to say about it, at the moment. Leave it to me."

Sir William eyed him curiously.

"You perhaps haven't noticed it, Mac?" he observed, "but there are a devil of a lot of things being left to you. I hope they pan out, all right, otherwise it may lead to awkward questions."

"It may indeed," McCarthy agreed complacently. "And if it should, you just leave the answers to those awkward questions to me. So long."

CHAPTER XIV

ENTER THE SIGNOR PIETRO SPEROZZA

IT was perhaps two hours later when a taxi-cab drew up outside McCarthy's Dean Street lodgings driven by as tough a person who had ever held a taxi-driver's licence; by name, Mr. William Withers.

He was a huge man with hands like ten pound hams, one magnificent specimen of cauliflower-ear and a nose that was very decidedly, and permanently, off the true. There were very few habitués of the West End of London, whether crook or straight, who did not know "Big Bill" Withers, and there were several who, having in a much-mistaken spirit of derring-do, endeavoured to bilk him for his fare, who would never forget him to the longest day they lived.

Just what the antecedents of "Big Bill" had been before joining the ranks of the taxi-driving fraternity was not commonly known to the public. He had been a burglar, for the prosecution of which gentle art he had done several terms of imprisonment.

Nor was the manner in which he had acquired his vehicle common knowledge. Detective-Inspector McCarthy, as well as a certain swell cracksman, known in the Underworld as "The Wall-flower" could have enlightened them, but as they chose to keep the matter a profound secret, no one was any the wiser.

But when the inspector had a job on hand which called for the services of a taxi-man of known steadiness and reliability, Mr. William Withers was invariably the person requisitioned.

Having been invoked by telephone from his combined home and garage in Clerkenwell, and having listened attentively to the instructions handed out by Inspector McCarthy, Mr. Withers repaired downstairs to his cab again and there waited for the coming of his patron. A little later a decidedly dubious-looking and unquestionably queer figure for the neighbourhood of Soho, slipped out of McCarthy's door and into the taxi-cab, to be speedily driven in the direction of Aldgate.

As to the clothing and general *tout ensemble* of this personage, it was by no means redolent of prosperity; indeed, very much the reverse. The whole exterior of the man was that of one who followed the sea in some capacity or other and, at the present moment, was very much down upon his luck. His costume consisted of a tattered blue jersey and splendidly oiled and ancient dungaree trousers, thrust into a pair of thigh-length sea-boots, the tops of which looped about his knees in the best approved buccaneer fashion. To carry on that simile, his very movement—a soundless mixture of cat-like tread and sailor-man roll—was typical of what he, himself, looked; desperado every inch of him. To make the picture still more complete, from under the peak of that cap, fierce dark eyes shot here and there, falling with an evil glare upon most humans who came within their compass. Very decidedly there was an *aura* of menace about the swarthy-visaged Signor Pietro Sperozza, sailorman, of Naples.

At the corner of the East India Dock Road he dispensed with Mr. Withers' services temporarily, but not before giving that worthy further final instructions to which "Big Bill" listened attentively, before starting back again for the West End. Then, with that wide sea-roll which told of one who had just come ashore after a long voyage, he started out for Limehouse and, from the first moment the pubs opened, began to drink himself into what appeared to be a state of acute and quarrelsome intoxication.

Not that this condition was any novelty to those denizens of Limehouse who had had previous acquaintance with the signor upon his trips to London. Upon most of his visits he generally finished up his first day in the cells of the Bow Road Police Station, and this occasion did not look as though it would be an exception to that rule.

As an actual matter of fact, it was at precisely nine o'clock when the signor, after leaving a dive in which he had consumed sufficient vile liquor to sink the proverbial ship, commenced to bawl at the top of his voice, and in the Italian language, an *aria* by the incomparable Puccini.

Upon being requested to cease the unmelodious row forthwith, he took the request as a national insult and drove his fist hard on the nose of the constable who made it. In less than five seconds the street was in an uproar; Chinese, white and half-caste dock-rats, street loungers, and tradesmen of all colours, seemingly vieing with each other as to who could make the most noise. Who they favoured in the contest it was impossible to tell.

Eventually it took six of the toughest members of the K. Division to get the signor sufficiently down to be strapped to a hand ambulance and in that manner he was removed to Limehouse Station. But the last the citizens of Limehouse saw of him, he was still bawling an excerpt from *Madame Butterfly* at the top of his anything but beautiful voice.

Perhaps an hour later Mr. Withers' taxi appeared and parked in an alley at the side of the station; after a wait of a few minutes the signor ducked out of a side-door and into it, and he was again driven back to the West End.

"Pick me up in Russell Square at midnight exactly, Withers," he instructed.

"I'll be there, sir, to the tick," that worthy assured him.

The hour had just struck when McCarthy, no longer apparelled in the garb of the pugnacious Pietro Sperozza, but in another make-up quite as distinctive, slouched into Russell Square and mooched along to where a taxi-cab was waiting.

"O.K., Withers," he said, as he passed, whereupon the burly driver set his cab in motion.

The Inspector crossed the square and disappeared into Museum Street, followed by the taxi. At the darkest point he could find he stood waiting until the cab came up to him.

"Now, Withers," he said in a low voice, "you quite understand the orders?"

"I think so, sir," "Big Bill" said. "I was to go on ahead of you into Fortescue Square and take a liker at the fourth house on the right to see if there are any signs of anyone on the watch, then drive through the Square, double back into the alley at the rear and pull up close to the wall. Then I take a mike around to see there's nobody 'anging about that side. If there is, I dots 'im one."

"Right, Withers," McCarthy said.

From his pocket "Big Bill" took what appeared to be a short piece of tubular steel but which was, in reality, a telescopic jemmy.

"It's small, guv'nor," he said, "but you could shift the door of a vault with this 'ere little article."

At a nod from McCarthy, Withers moved on and made for Fortescue Square, followed at a distance by the Inspector. The Square was quite empty and McCarthy was gratified to see the back of the policeman on beat just turning the corner on his way out of it. That meant he would have at least half an hour before there would be any likelihood of police interference.

He shuffled past the head of the square, giving not so much as a glance towards Professor Farman's house, but one upward flick of his eyes showed him that there was a light in that room from which Miss Ridley had watched him. Whatever had been the cause of her sudden fear she was evidently all right up to this point.

In the alley he found Withers waiting with all lights out. He reported that everything was clear.

From the top of Withers' cab McCarthy negotiated that formidable glass-topped wall with ease; a moment later saw him upon the roof of the long out-house which ran up to the residence itself.

"Keep your eyes wide open, Withers," he cautioned. "I've an idea that the Egyptian servants here are a tough handful, and anything may happen the moment I get into the place."

"The one that gets a tap over the nut with my spanner won't be so tough after it," Mr. Withers assured him sturdily.

Stretched out, McCarthy went along the shed roof with the ease of a cat over tiles. At the end of it, he found that the window which he had decided to work from was a good three feet above his reach, but that, fortunately, there was a down-pipe from the roof which ran within a foot of it. Testing this, he found it solid, and in the darkness of the night there was not a great deal of chance of his being seen. The brickwork was old and rough, and promised every chance of sufficient toe-hold; actually it was a matter of seconds before he found himself upon the sill and got to work with Withers' jemmy.

With, the expertness of a cat-burglar, he manipulated the catch with which the window was fastened, lifted it noiselessly, and crept inside. He found himself in a long corridor from which, his masked torch showed him, opened several doors.

The house itself was as still as though it had been two o'clock in the morning instead of a little past twelve; either its inhabitants, with the exception of Miss Ridley, were out, or the household retired early. He devoutly hoped, for the success of his purpose, that it was the former. Especially was he anxious to find Miss Ridley's room and slip under her door a short note of reassurance which he had written before leaving his lodgings.

Each of the rooms proved to be a bedroom, and apparently, untenanted. At the end of this corridor he came to another which traversed it and ended in a staircase which led upstairs. It was at this point that a strange, pungent scent began to assail his nostrils. He had encountered it many times before among the dens and dives of Limehouse and the river-front, and knew it instantly to be the reek of *opium*! Someone quite close to him was either smoking, or had finished, a pipe, and was, in all probability, lost in the ecstatic bliss of the opium-smoker's dreams!

It came from, he discovered, a room upon his right hand which, upon trial, proved to be locked. Taking his pick-lock from his pocket, he inserted it and, slowly and noiselessly, turned the lock.

For a few moments he stood still, waiting to see if any sound came from the room, but it remained as silent as the rest of the house.

Slowly he turned the handle and opened the door a foot or two, to be almost driven back by the reek and the acrid smoke that filled his eyes. There was no necessity for him to use his torch to see that the semi-naked figure sprawled upon the bed was Professor Farman!

CHAPTER XV

WHICH TELLS HOW McCARTHY HAS A NARROW ESCAPE, BUT LEFT STILL GREATER TROUBLE BEHIND HIM

FOR a moment utter revulsion held McCarthy rigid, then his eyes began to wander about the room. Upon a low table covered by an Egyptian-brass tray stood, lit, the peanut-oil lamp by which the devotees of the poppy cook their opium pills. Upon the tray, also, lay some three or four opium-pipes of magnificent carving and workmanship. Nearby, and upon which McCarthy's eyes fixed avidly, was a small, circular box in which were four pills ready for smoking. In a flash the lid was on the box and it was transferred to his pocket.

From the table his eyes went to that semi-naked figure sprawled upon the bed. The very sight of it turned him sick with utter disgust. Gone were all traces of Professor Farman's former dignity; the face which stared sightlessly at the ceiling, devoid of any sign of intelligence, might have belonged to any one of the lowest possible strata of mankind. The clutching fingers, the twitching limbs, were no longer those of a man of the highest intellect, but an animal, rendered so by the drug to which he was a slave. In a flash the situation as he now saw it filled McCarthy with a great fear for the girl under this roof! That such a situation as existed could have been possible had never entered his head, but what was before his eyes left him in no possible doubt as to her very genuine danger.

If this were the head of the household, what of the rest—those five Egyptians who had followed him through all his wanderings and were now somewhere ensconced in the darkness of this sinister house? Nothing was more certain than that they, too, would be opium addicts, as was their master, and in the midst of them, absolutely helpless from attack, this beautiful, pure young girl, whose mind knew no evil. Small wonder that she felt fear; her natural instinct had warned her only too rightly of danger.

More than ever he felt compelled to give her some message to keep up her courage. Before he made a move to explore that mysterious museum in which Farman and the five servants worked alone in complete secrecy, he must pass to her the little note he had scribbled before leaving his lodgings, intending to slip it under her door. She would see it the first thing in the morning, if not before that. As soon as it was possible he would see that she had sufficient protection, though just how he was going to do it was, for the moment, beyond him.

As he crept up the stairs, keeping to the outside of the treads that there might be no creak from them, the thought was strong in his mind that this mystery man, this Jung Dorasso, as Miss Ridley had called him, was the only one beside the professor and his servants who was allowed into that museum. What would a search of that room reveal?

As soon as he had concluded the comedy of the morning in Bow Police Court and made it possible for the Signor Pietro Sperozza to invade Wan How's main den without suspicion, he would give his whole attention to this house. That something was radically wrong here he was quite certain—if it were not so why had the professor lied upon the point of not knowing who the man was who had accosted him in the British Museum and, still more, kept entirely to himself the fact, inadvertently let out by Miss Ridley, that this Jung Dorasso had been in the house right up to the moment of Grey's departure to his death.

The professor would kick up a devil of a fuss when any mention of official search of the house was made; would present a picture of truly outraged dignity—if nothing more belligerent. But all his indignation, or argument, could not do away with the fact of those four opium-pills, and also that, from some source or other, he was acquiring the drug, if only for his own use.

Continuing up, he came to a landing which he judged to be at the elevation of her room. From under the one door which opened from it, there came a faint gleam of light; without hesitation, he stooped and pushed the little missive under it.

That instinct of self-preservation which had saved him in more than one tight corner, stood him in good stead once more. He swerved swiftly and, as he did so a curved scimitar, wielded by the stockily-built Ali, whistled over his shoulder and buried itself in the woodwork of the door. It came with terrific force and he heard the girl's startled cry as the weapon ripped into the timber. Then, like lightning, he went into action!

Rushing at the dark shadow which he could now see was a human form, he smashed his cast-iron fist against the Egyptian's jaw, sending the brown man reeling into a corner. But before he could even turn, Ali had recovered and was at him like a wild-cat, endeavouring to get to grips for a wrestling-hold. Knowing full well what masters of that sport many Egyptians were, and equally realising the strength of his opponent, McCarthy was forced to put forth every effort to finish his attacker quickly. His first thought was to prevent the other uttering a cry that would bring his fellows to his aid.

With terrible swiftness and the directness of piston-rods his fists flashed into the Egyptian's face, cutting it to ribbons. But it seemed that he could take punishment which would have speedily finished many another man. All the time, although McCarthy's blows brought grunts from him, he was still striving to get the hold he wanted. Then, suddenly, the Scotland Yard man landed one desperate blow under the ear which dropped the Egyptian to his knees; in the next instant McCarthy was flying down those stairs again and making for the window by which he had entered.

But, terrific as had been the blow Ali had received, it was yet not sufficient to keep him down. McCarthy had not reached the bottom of the first flight of stairs before he was up, had torn the scimitar from the door, and hurled it!

But, after the terrible battering he had received, and half blinded, his aim was again erratic—the heavy steel blade flew wide and smashed into a large Oriental mirror which shivered into a thousand pieces with a terrible crash.

"That," McCarthy thought grimly, "is going to bring the whole hornets' nest down upon me."

As he shot into the cross-passage, the door of that reeking room where he had left the professor opened, and Farman, a ghastly-looking object, stumbled out. In his hand he carried a heavy automatic pistol which, without hesitation, he levelled at the flying figure. Instantly McCarthy dived for the semi-doped man's knees, and the bullet whined over his head and struck a wall with a heavy thud.

Swinging the professor off his feet bodily, McCarthy tossed him back through the open door and heard him crash down upon that littered table.

From below, now, he could hear the excited jabber of the other Egyptians, followed by the drawing of heavy bolts; some of them, still under the spell of their opium-pipes, had made the mistake of thinking that the disturbance was outside and were making for the yard.

Along the corridor he sped, vaulted through the window, and dropped on to the roof of the outhouse with one movement. As he did so two of the Egyptians rushed out from the shed beneath him and kept pace with him as he ran along the roof to that glass-topped back wall. With one spring he cleared it and landed upon the top of Withers' taxi-cab.

"Go, Limehouse!" he hissed as he dropped upon his hands and knees and clung on. Before the Egyptians could get the wooden door to the alley open, the taxi-cab was careering down its length at the best pace its owner could knock out of it. Nor did he ease down until he discovered that his patron was climbing down the side and endeavouring to get the door open! By that time they were nearly back in Russell Square.

"Lime'us, you said, sir," "Big Bill" said inquiringly. "Is that a alteration of the orders?"

"No," McCarthy said. "In the excitement of the moment I'd completely forgotten that I'd got to change to go down there before I can appear in the dock in the morning, and, moreover, Withers, that was a dam' bad break of mine, letting out the word, 'Lime-house.' Let us hope those Egyptians can't understand English. Get back to Soho till I change into my sailor duds."

"Was the job a failure, sir?" Mr. Withers asked commiseratingly.

"Yes—and no, Withers. I went to run the rule over a certain room in that house and I never got anywhere near it. But I picked up something else that may prove of tremendous value to me."

"You can't 'ave it both ways, sir," "Big Bill" said philosophically. "If you get it on the swings, you drop it on the roundabouts. That's 'ow things goes in this world."

In the house in Fortescue Square, the professor, although half-stunned, was shaking off the effects of the opium and was endeavouring to make sense of what the blood-bespattered Ali was jabbering at him. Slowly it began to percolate through his brain that, whoever the intruder had been, it seemed that the girl above was one of his primary interests. Ali told him of the paper which had been pushed beneath her door.

At the information the professor's face went livid with rage.

"Bring her down, and the paper," he ordered with a gesture upwards, then turned for a moment back into his room.

Strangely enough, the peanut-oil lamp was still burning where it had fallen on the floor, and, lifting it, his bleared eyes searched the room in its dim light. Then replacing the lamp, with his one hand he felt among the scattered articles still upon the table. His teeth bared in an ugly snarl when he realised that the opium-pills and their box had gone.

Whatever the savage and sinister thoughts passing through his mind, they were broken into by the appearance of Ali and one of the Egyptians dragging between them the terrified girl. In her fingers was still gripped the note she had, but a moment or two before, picked up from the floor.

Snatching it from her, the professor scanned its contents, and the ugly scowl upon his face deepened.

"So!" he snarled. "It would seem that you are in league with those who seek to cause me trouble."

"I do not understand you," the girl cried. "Tell these men to let me go. They are hurting me."

"If that is all the harm they do you," he returned in a voice loaded with menace, "you will have escaped lightly. This amply proves to me that you are not to be trusted. You have had some communication with this McCarthy apart from what I have been informed of. Well, I will put you where you can do him no good, and myself no harm."

At a sign from him, Ali clapped a cloth over the girl's mouth and bound it tightly, then, struggling wildly, she was lifted from the ground and borne downstairs, through the basement to the cellars.

The one into which she was roughly flung was so thickly walled that no sound that she could make would ever be heard outside it.

The professor was still muttering viciously to himself when the two who had been out, rushed back and reported.

"Limehouse?" he echoed when he had heard the order McCarthy had given. "Is that destination pure coincidence, or . . . something else? Why Limehouse, just on the eve of—"

He broke off and lapsed into thought for a moment.

"It is too great a danger to be accepted as pure chance," he muttered. "I must warn them all."

He made his way to the hall and dialled a number upon the telephone there, then waited. A few moments later the thin, cracked voice of the notorious den-keeper, Wan How, came across the wire to him. For a full three minutes he spoke earnestly to that arch-scoundrel. When at last he rang off there was a satisfied smile upon his still-twitching face.

"If our nocturnal visitor, Inspector McCarthy, does go to Limehouse upon the prowl, he will be a lucky man, indeed, if ever he comes out of it again."

Restlessly he began to pace the hall.

"Assuming that he has those opium-pills, what can he prove by them? No more than that I, in common with so many Eastern travellers, am an opium-addict. Possession of the drug is a misde-meanour, doubtless, but, even if charged with it, I need implicate no one else. I can swear upon my last visit I brought a supply back, sufficient to last me for years. But this accursed girl of Ridley's whom I kept by me purely as a safeguard may turn out to be a bigger menace than ever I could have believed possible. Who can say what she has, or has not, seen in this house without us being any the wiser? She must be got away at once, before morning, if possible, to where her tongue can work no more mischief."

Again he went to the 'phone and dialled. Within two minutes of his leaving the instrument a closed car containing a driver and three other Egyptians was speeding from Caversham to Fortescue Square.

CHAPTER XVI

SIGNOR PIETRO SPEROZZA PAYS SOME VISITS

THAT curious habit of the Chinese of attending almost any form of free entertainment from a public and political meeting of which they could not understand a word, to the Salvation Army barracks, was well at the back of Inspector McCarthy's mind when he thought out the return of Pietro Sperozza to the docklands.

He was as positive that the Bow Road Police Court would have among its audience a very solid sprinkling of the yellow men, treating the whole show very much as if it were a theatre. Amongst them also, he was equally well aware, would be one or two of old Wan How's spies; what happened in the police court was generally of considerable interest to that old scoundrel, although he never put in personal appearance there himself.

One glance around the court as he took his stand in the dock showed him that his judgment had been perfectly correct; there they were, right enough, and listening intently to every word that was uttered.

Upon his appearance, several of the yellow brotherhood who had doubtless been present at the scrimmage of the previous evening bent their heads together and whispered quickly. From what he could see of it, he was the stellar attraction, in-so-far as the Chinamen went at any rate. Which was exactly what he wanted; within a few minutes of his being dealt with every word in his case would have been reported to Wan How.

He was arraigned by a solemn-looking Inspector upon a serious charge; to wit, that he had, upon the night previous when under the influence of drink, first constituted himself a public nuisance by singing at the top of his voice in the street and alternating this by challenging male passers-by to a fight.

Upon being warned by Police Constable Michael O'Shea as to the seriousness of his conduct, he, in the language of the police witness, "hauled off" and struck the officer upon the nose.

Constable O'Shea, coming himself from a world-renowned fighting family (the O'Shea's, County Wexford, Ireland) promptly responded to this indignity by punching the signor in the eye. After a fierce combat, and with the aid of several other constables and a hand-ambulance, Signor Sperozza was taken into custody. He had likewise injured the officer's uniform by tearing off a button.

Had Pietro Sperozza anything to say for himself?

He had. It was, he explained, the change from the wine of his native Naples to the beer of England which was responsible for the catastrophe. He had, but the afternoon before, come ashore from the good ship, *Comendatore Rossi*, upon which vessel he was a stoker, and, at the time of the opening of the licensed houses, partaken of a few pints of beer. After which he had very little, indeed, *no* recollection of subsequent happenings. All he knew was that when he woke up in the cell this morning he was in a stiff and sore state and the possessor of one eye which refused to open—said eye pointed out to the Stipendiary and unquestionably one of the finest specimens of discoloured optics ever seen in that court.

Signor Sperozza offered the most handsome apologies all round, and gratuitously promised that the offence would not be repeated. The Inspector of police then offered some gratuitous information! He informed the magistrate that over a period of years, no greater nuisance had ever entered the Port of London than the man at present in the dock. When he was not drinking, he was fighting, and the only time he refrained from either one or the other, or both, was when he was in the cells.

Signor Sperozza, after a terse lecture from the magistrate, was fined forty shillings or a month, and was further informed that the next time he made appearance in that court upon the same charge he would be dealt with with much greater severity.

Bowing affably not only to the stipendiary but also to those seated in the body of the court, including his Chinese audience, Signor Sperozza descended from the dock, pulled a bundle of frowsy-looking notes from a pocket of his tattered coat, paid his fine, and departed with all the braggadocio of a great adventurer.

He first moved to a little public-house in a back street at some distance from the court, and there waited. Some five minutes later he was joined by the officer who had charged him and the Inspector who had blackened his name and good fame.

"Thanks, boys," he said when the drinks had been ordered. "You did it splendidly, both last night and this morning. It's just the entrance I wanted into Chinatown. Those slant eyes of theirs are getting so keen that it wants something to back up a make-up to get away with it. I knew the court would be full of Chinks. It always is."

"I'm sorry about that eye, Inspector," Constable O'Shea mentioned apologetically.

"Don't fret about that," McCarthy said. "If I hadn't wanted it, I shouldn't have got it. It just tops off what I'm vain enough to think a corking good disguise. And, anyhow, as my first visit is to an old doctor, it's just as well to have something that wants mending. He can start on this eye."

"D'ye mean old Doctor Quong See?" the Inspector inquired.

"The same," McCarthy replied.

"He's a friend of yours, isn't he?"

"When I'm in plain clothes—yes," McCarthy answered.

"D'ye think he won't know you?" the Inspector asked.

McCarthy grinned:

"Did you two until you got me into the cells?" he parried quizzically.

"No, I'm damned if we did," the Inspector answered—and meant it.

"Then we'll hope he doesn't," the Scotland Yard man said, "because I'm after big game this time."

When Inspector McCarthy arrived at the modest little shop whereat the venerable Doctor Quong See dispensed his herbs and other remedies, he found the space before the counter full. A Chinese woman, nursing a wailing baby, was the first to be attended to, after which a chubby-faced Chinese girl of perhaps six or seven years produced from the capacious sleeve of her tunic a small puppy which, it appeared, had to have a broken leg set.

Quong See bowed deeply to the disreputable-looking newcomer.

"Pray be seated, honourable sir," he said in the thin, worn voice of extreme age and indicating a chair with his tiny, claw-like hands.

McCarthy sat down and viewed the proceedings, though he was far more interested in watching the face of the old man who might easily have been called the good shepherd of his poorer countrymen. It fascinated him.

From his face alone it would have been impossible to compute his actual years, for he had long passed the stage of life when the features give any true indication of age. The whole head was absolutely hairless, the skin like old ivory-vellum stretched tightly over the bones, and scored with thousands upon thousands of wrinkles.

But the shrunken-lipped, heavily-scored mouth was firmly set, and in the oblique, jet-black eyes which looked through modern, tortoise-shell glasses, there was nothing of weakness of mind or senility; nothing, indeed, but the imperishable wisdom of all the ages. Strange eyes they were, those of Quong See; the pupils, fathomless in depth—utterly inscrutable. Unblinking eyes, that fixed with piercing penetration upon whoever they turned, that seemed to read down into the most hidden recesses of the minds of men. Yet in their depths there seemed to dwell a kindly light that spoke of inherent gentleness.

He was dressed in a long robe of blue jean, so cheap that it might have been worn by the poorest coolie, but about his waist was a yellow girdle which, though McCarthy did not know it, marked him as the descendant in line of an Emperor, while the yellow button on the top of his threadbare skull-cap told of high services rendered to the state during the dynasty of the Manchus.

The woman, having been provided with her medicines, departed without any offer of payment, McCarthy noted. But in the doorway she turned and made the old doctor an obeisance that might have been given to a monarch.

Quong See then turned his attention to the puppy and in very little time, under his skilful fingers, its plaintive whimperings ceased. But where, in the case of the woman, Quong See had scarcely uttered a word, he kept up a conversation with the child and in a dialect which the Scotland Yard man knew to be quite different from the ordinary Cantonese of Chinatown. What he had to say must have been of tremendous interest to the little one, for she kept bobbing her pig-tailed head vigorously, though her little amber-coloured face was about as tell-tale as that of the Sphinx, itself, and her black, lashless eyes as inscrutable as those of the venerable doctor himself.

She and her charge disposed of, Quong See turned to the ragamuffin figure in the chair inquiringly.

McCarthy got up.

"I getta inna da fight," he was beginning, when, with a slight gesture of the claw-like hands, the doctor stopped him and held open a heavy curtain at the entrance to an inner room.

"Be pleased to walk inside my lowly room, honourable sir," he said quietly, an invitation which McCarthy instantly accepted. Once inside and the curtain drawn to, he began again.

"Inna da fight I get dese," he said, touching his contused eye gingerly.

Quong See bowed, waved his hand towards a chair which McCarthy took and busied himself, pouring certain unguents into quaint little bowls upon which were Chinese hieroglyphics.

"It is a strange thing, a matter of world history, how deeply ingrained the love of personal battle is in your people, Inspector," he observed casually.

"Eh!" McCarthy ejaculated, completely taken aback by the quick perception of the old man who had scarcely given him a glance from the moment he entered the door.

"But it is equally strange that a man of your knowledge and experience should not perceive at once that the face and the clothes of a man are only a very small part of his general characteristics. In fact, among the least of them. You, yourselves, in your detective system, admit that. You dare not depend upon faces to incriminate a man—human types are reproduced too often. Hence you rely upon something which is never duplicated twice; the whorls of the finger-tips."

"True enough," McCarthy was forced to admit with a sigh.

"Now I," went on Quong See placidly, "have many times noticed that a certain friend of mine has what must have been once a deep cut at the edge of the nail of his right hand index-finger, probably made by the knife-point of some criminal with whom he was engaged. A man enters my shop, I glance at his eyes to find in the one really visible, an expression with which I am well acquainted—another thing unalterable. It is the habitual expression of that friend of whom I speak. I glance at his hands, and there, at the side of that nail, is the tell-tale scar which tells me that it is that friend, beyond any possibility of doubt."

"I'd like to know just how much you really do know of men, and things, and human nature, generally," McCarthy said ruefully.

The doctor did not answer for a moment, but applied himself to McCarthy's injured eye. "A severe blow," he commented.

"The fellow who did it hits like the kick of a mule," McCarthy agreed.

Quong See passed out through the curtain, and McCarthy heard him close the outer door of the shop. In a moment he returned and went on with his administrations.

"Why are you here, my friend?" he asked.

"Because I want some advice from you—and help. There has been a murder committed, a brutal murder in the West End; Bloomsbury, to be exact. That, again was followed by one at Reading, and there is little doubt that both were committed by the same people."

"I know neither place," the old doctor said quietly and also with a significance in his voice McCarthy could not miss.

"I know that," the Inspector said, "but it all seems to hinge upon one thing that you do know quite a lot about, Doctor Quong See—opium."

"Are Chinese people believed to be implicated in it?" the doctor asked quickly.

McCarthy smiled grimly.

"There you go," he said, " 'Are Chinese people believed to be implicated in it?' And if they were, not one syllable to help could I ever get out of you, honest and law-abiding citizen as I know you to be, and a man utterly incapable of any evil yourself. The moment it becomes a case of white versus yellow, we come up against the Great and Impenetrable Silence. No one knows anything; no one has heard, still less seen anything. There's nothing but the blank wall. In that, you're just like my mother's people, the Italians. Let the *Maffia* or the *Camorista* do one of their executions in Soho or Saffron Hill, and we're up against exactly the same thing. No one's seen, no one's heard; no one knows anything."

For a moment the old doctor regarded him gravely.

"I am still waiting an answer to my question," he reminded.

"The answer is, no," McCarthy told him. "So far as I'm aware, there's no question, or even suggestion, that the Chinese have anything whatever to do with either crime."

Doctor Quong See made a little gesture with his thin hands.

"In that case, my friend," he said, "I am at your service. What is the advice you seek from me?"

From his pocket, McCarthy took the small box containing the four opium pills he had taken from the table by the bedside of Professor Farman and handed them over.

"Doctor," he said, "I know that you are not an opium-smoker —that, indeed, you hold the practice in great abhorrence."

"That is quite true," Doctor Quong See returned. "I have seen it ruin my own country, though, I am bound to say, through no fault of its own. Had it not been for the drugs sent out freely by the foreign concessions and, therefore, untouchable by the Chinese authorities, opium would have been wiped out of China years ago."

"I want to know," McCarthy asked, "just what is this particular sample. Indian, Chinese, Egyptian, or Macedonian?"

Quong See ran one of his shrivelled fingers over one of the little pills, then tasted it.

"Egyptian," he pronounced unhesitatingly. "Moreover, Egyptian of a very high grade. A year or two ago a drug of this quality rarely came into this country, my friend—not even into the hands of the medical men. But it has been getable here in greater or smaller quantities for some little time. If I wanted it, I should not have to go very far to procure it."

"You mean Wan How?" McCarthy asked eagerly.

The thin, old shoulders elevated in a shrug.

"To ask too many questions, my friend, is not wisdom," he said quietly. "To answer them, still less so!"

CHAPTER XVII

AT WAN HOW'S!

AS might have been expected—and, indeed, had been banked upon by the Inspector—the advent of Signor Sperozza after his pitched battle of the night before, and police-court experience of the morning, was heartily welcomed by that portion of Chinatown which is dominated by gangland.

But, singularly enough for a person of his curiously mercurial temperament, the signor took the day very quietly—it was almost as though the warning words of the stipendiary magistrate had been emitted to some purpose. He confined himself to an exceedingly subdued round of some of the quieter hostelries where nothing but the real Simon Pure sailormen congregated and, indeed, took his pleasures somewhat sadly.

For some hours during the afternoon, he disappeared completely, but at dark he was back in the quarter again and seemed to have recovered some little of his usually high spirits.

What McCarthy did not know, and it would have given him furiously to think, had he been aware of it, was the fact that his every movement up to that mysterious disappearance, was being shadowed by two of Wan How's half-caste dock-rats. They had been present at his public pillorying in the police court, and from then on trailed him everywhere he went, reporting in to the yellow boss they stood in mortal terror of by means of runners.

Within a few minutes of his visit to Quong See, the fact was known to Wan How, who, in that underground room which he sometimes alluded to as an "office" but which no one but the very elect of his workers ever entered, thought over the visit very seriously indeed.

True, it was equally reported to him that undoubtedly the sailor-man's eye had been attended to by the old medical man—that fact was obvious. But still—

A certain telephone message Wan How had received in the early hours of the morning had not tended in any degree to lessen his suspicion of every person who entered Chinatown. True, the signor had created his disturbance there the night before and had been promptly incarcerated. That seemed clear enough, but the cunning mind of the opium-runner and white-slave dealer saw traps everywhere.

Moreover, there was no love in Wan How's heart for his fellow-countryman, the aged Doctor Quong See. The doctor was too great an influence for good among the respectable members of the community; indeed, he was as powerful among them as Wan How was among the completely opposite section. In particular, he was anti-opium to what Wan How considered to be a fanatic degree. But for Doctor Quong See's exhortations, in season and out, against the drug, many thousands of pounds would have come into his already over-swollen coffers which the doctor had diverted.

Had Wan How had his way, he would have had the venerable Quong See kidnapped and put him to a death in those catacombs beneath his premises beside which that of A Thousand Slices would have been a joke. And, moreover, the ex-Cantonese coolie would have sat and chuckled at the agonies of one whom he knew to be an aristocrat, born in the purple.

There was one other reason why Wan How had not long before rid himself of the pestilent Quong See, and that reason was all-sufficing to a man who had amassed money and could afford himself the delights of the earth. It was that, from sources not to be doubted, he had learned that Doctor Quong See was the virtual head in England of that all-powerful Chinese secret society, the Tong of a Million Eyes. And that it was really all-powerful Wan How had the best of all reasons for believing. Its word was law to at least seventy-five per cent. of the full-blooded Chinese in England, and the famous Bim Kong Tong, of New York, and the Hip Sing Tong, of San Francisco, were merely branches of the mother-tong which had its centre in Shanghai—some said in Pekin, itself. The Tong which boasted that it had a million eyes to watch for its enemies and a million hands to mete out punishment.

Fatalist, even as he was, the last thing Wan How wanted was to find himself in the hands of the Tong of a Million Eyes, particularly after anything untoward had happened to the venerated Quong See, *and* that happening could be traced to him.

But there was one other thing Wan How knew, and that was that a certain man whose name had been whispered over the telephone to him but the night before was a big friend of the doctor's; a man who, of all persons connected with law and order, he hated more than any ten others. Detective-Inspector McCarthy.

Only too well had he cause to know the artifices of almost Oriental cunning which the Inspector was wont to use in the trapping of criminals, either yellow or white. He knew that upon many occasions the dreaded McCarthy had received help from Quong See when the criminals had been other than Chinese. That the Italian sailor-man should have gone straight from the police court to Quong See was a matter of suspicion—anyone who went to Quong See just at this present juncture came under suspicion.

Sitting there and thinking over the Italian sailor's past sporadic visits to Chinatown and the docklands generally, it seemed to Wan How that the dates of those visits seemed to coincide in an extraordinary way with extremely unhappy events which followed. The more he thought it over, the more certain in his mind he became that Sperozza, if not connected with the hated Scotland Yard directly, was one of those agents who nosed out and took them information—hence the strange appellation by which they were known: police "noses."

But upon one thing Wan How had quite made up his mind—let Inspector McCarthy set foot in the docklands after his raid upon the Fortescue Square house the night before, and he would never go out of it again alive. There had been no doubt whatever that Limehouse was the direction the Professor's Egyptian servants had heard him give, and, to Wan How, Limehouse meant only one thing—Wan How, and one or other of his establishments.

Not that he meant having any hand in it himself. The police were quite difficult enough in the ordinary way without having any charges of that kind up their sleeve. But there were others in the vicinity and on the watch for him; men not even of Chinese origin, who, if they attacked and finished a man, it could not possibly be laid at the door of Wan How.

Still, it would be very easy to drop the Egyptians from "up the river" a quiet hint that Signor Sperozza might very well be picked up and dealt with later, if he were found to be other than he seemed.

With which decision, and an order to his men to redouble their vigilant watch over all strangers in Chinatown, he was forced to be content. He did not like the Italian sailorman's strange disappearance during the afternoon, but doubtless he would be back again with nightfall; he would not be given a second chance to disappear, at any rate not beyond the ken of Wan How.

McCarthy, during that disappearance, had laid quite a few things in train. For one, he had had a close watch set upon Professor Farman's house, with particular instruction that the professor, should he leave it, was to be watched every moment of the time. In particular, one man was assigned to watch a certain room high up in that house and, should a young lady be observed there, endeavour to pass to her some signal by which she might know that there were friends around her. After that, he issued certain instructions to "Big Bill" Withers.

"Find the nearest open garage to Wan How's and fill up your tank. We may have a long run after I'm there. Park your car as near to his dive as is possible and where you can be sure that it won't be run off with. You're known at Wan How's, aren't you?"

"They know me, all right, down there," Mr. Withers assured him.

"Then drop in there casually and mark a few tickets for the lottery," McCarthy instructed. "That will give you the excuse for stopping there until it's drawn. But make no mistake about one thing—don't recognise me in any shape or form or, indeed, come near me at all. I'll give you the office when to clear out and wait for me."

It was nearly ten o'clock that night when, after a few drinks at different places about the neighbourhood (sufficient to let Wan How's scouts know that he was back in Limehouse as he was well aware they would do) that he dropped into that unsavoury rendezvous alone. By that time, the Signor Pietro Sperozza, although unusually subdued, was fairly well gone in liquor.

One glance around showed him that the place was extraordinarily full, and that, in a large inner room, the gambling at *fan-tan*, *py-gow*, and *hie-goot-pie* was in progress. Over in that far corner of the main room where the lottery was conducted was a crowd of every nationality and colour, amongst whom the huge form of "Big Bill" Withers towered.

He also noted that gangland was in particularly good strength to-night; most of the "pick-tips" and decoys, male and female, of the river-side plunderers being in evidence. It was unusual to find them all there, but they were quiet enough—Wan How's half-castes and full-blooded yellows, were a nasty lot to tackle once a row started under his roof.

He was somewhat surprised at the unctuous greeting accorded him by Wan How, but came to the conclusion that the fairly bulky wad of notes he had displayed in the court that morning had been reported to the old scoundrel. He meant having his cut first—others of similar kidney could have his leavings, if any.

At one table there sat a group of Argentines, cattle men just paid off from a River Plate refrigerator-boat. Among them he lurched, hailed them in their native Portuguese, bought a drink, and, en-sconcing himself comfortably, began to take a covert look around.

Over all the place, despite the fact that it was clouded in a pall of smoke and reeked of the vilest tobacco, hung that same acrid smell which had pervaded the professor's house. Somewhere at the back, or even—with the Chinese genius for cutting catacombs—deep beneath them, were the opium-dens which never, in any police raid, had ever been discovered. By hook or by crook, McCarthy meant getting at them to-night if it were humanly possible.

Somewhere there was a join-up between this Jung Durasso and Wan How. That had been amply proved by the Egyptian's visit to this very place, as reported by the dead Fox. That join-up could only be, as far as he could see, in connection with the opium Wan How was known to traffic in.

There was one door upon which McCarthy had his eyes fixed in especial; a roughly-boarded structure which, apparently, led no-where, since it appeared to be flush with that side of the wall which faced the river.

Excusing himself to his newly-found Argentino friends, he lurched across to where the ticket-markers for the late lottery were congregating. Catching Withers' eye, he gave that worthy a glance which was to be interpreted as "Get out as soon as possible and stand by!"

Then he reeled on to the bar itself, bought himself a drink, and, in the very act, discovered something—or thought he did.

To make certain, he crossed, drink in hand, to another part of the room to where a frowsy-looking white woman was endeavouring to persuade a drunken Scandinavian sailor, a blonde giant, to take her somewhere else, probably home. From that point he lurched to a table where some Americans were playing euchre, and, from that, to the *fan-tan* game. After which he left his drink at one end of the bar, passed along its length, and ordered another drink at the other, then repaired to the table nearest to the door in which he was in-terested.

But by that time, he had quite satisfied himself upon one point—that Wan How's little black, oblique eyes were watching him as a cat might watch a mouse. Why?

CHAPTER XVIII

THE MAN WITH THE SNOW-WHITE HAIR!

THE discovery that Wan How was taking any particular interest in him came as a surprise, and an unpleasantly disconcerting one, to McCarthy. Upon his previous visits, the wily old scoundrel had taken no more notice of him, personally, than he did any other drunken sailor-man who came there to be rooked, in some form or other, of his hard-earned money.

Had the Signor Sperozza become too obstreperous, or hilarious, a nod, or even a glint of the eyes in his direction from the Chinaman would very soon have had him attended to by some of those half-caste thugs who seemed to be waiting for just such jobs in every angle of the torturous building.

But upon this occasion there was no mistaking the fact that, despite his police-court publicity, the Signor Sperozza was being kept under the personal observation of the gang-boss, himself. No matter where McCarthy moved, or to what he gave an apparently maudlin attention, those oblique black eyes were fixed upon him. They did not even move from their objective when "Big Bill" Withers disengaged himself from the crowd around the lottery and made for the door; even though he spoke with the burly taxi-driver his eyes never left McCarthy.

"You no wlait for lottery?" he inquired, amiably.

"No can do," Withers answered with a friendly grin he was far from feeling. "Got a job on—savvy? Look back later, p'raps. If I don't," he concluded, "you can bank my winnings for me in me maiden name. So long."

"*Hoki*," Wan How returned. He had not the faintest idea of what Mr. Withers' humour was about, but with Wan How "*Hoki*" was a sufficient answer to anything.

"Big Bill" gone, McCarthy scanned the faces of those about the place, endeavouring to pick such of them as had the earmarks of the opium-addict. Close attention to one of them might reveal something. But he took particularly good care to do so in the blear-eyed and casual manner befitting one who, although he had no personal interest in them, had arrived at that stage of drunken felicity which made him brother to all men.

His gaze fell eventually upon one man who, from his powerful physical proportions, McCarthy would not have put down as a day more than forty, but whose sun-blackened face was topped by as thick a stubble of wiry-looking white hair as ever he had seen. It was cut square and stood up on his head like an inverted scrubbing-brush.

But it was the man's deep-set, restless eyes and generally impatient manner which interested McCarthy most. He, too, appeared to be taking keen stock of all present and continually eyed the door; certainly no one either came in or went out of it who did not receive his concentrated attention. He wore the ordinary togs of a sea-going man, but upon the table near him lay a heavy walking-stick which could more easily have claimed the title of cudgel.

But for his poverty of dress, he could quite well have been one of the old school of iron-fisted windjammer captains, but as, with his hard, direct glance and complete absence of any sign of physical or mental shakiness, he looked about the last man in the world to be an opium-addict, McCarthy eventually dismissed him from his mind.

He noticed, though, that man was eyeing him curiously, almost as though he were trying to make out for his own satisfaction just what variety of sea-going clown the much-talked of Sperozza was. McCarthy found himself thinking with grim amusement that the Sperozzas of this world would have had an extremely rough passage on board any ship that the white-haired man was in command of.

It becoming more plain every moment that, under the watchful scrutiny of Wan How, his chance of investigating that door from the inside was going to be exactly nil, he determined to have a shot at it from the exterior. Casually he got up and, mumbling in Italian as he went, made an uncertain way towards the main entrance. As he passed the white-haired man he found himself being favoured by a singularly searching look from that worthy; an attention of which he took no notice whatever.

At the actual exit, he found one of Wan How's full-blooded yellows lounging, and he, too, favoured the detective with a hard glance—unusual, indeed, for one so well known there as the man he represented was purported to be. After he had passed him, a glance back showed McCarthy that the yellow man had stolen silently across the floor to Wan How and was speaking earnestly to his employer. But Wan How, although listening keenly, moved not a muscle of his face and remained perfectly still.

The exterior of that particular portion of Wan How's cunningly interlocked dens of iniquity faced a small, cobbled-stoned triangle, which again opened out on to the Thames. Once out in this space, McCarthy found that a weak moon had broken through scudding clouds, shedding just sufficient light to make objects both ashore and on the water fairly clear.

In front of him was the broad sweep of the river at high tide, and almost opposite, a biggish liner was slowly making her way up to her berth in the nearby docks. Smaller craft were on the move up and down in plenty, the chirpy toots from their sirens contrasting, almost humorously, with the deep and hoarse bellow which came from the liner. Out in mid-stream were to be seen the bellied sails of deeply-loaded barges making their way up upon the tide.

He was about to turn into a narrow alley which ran between the waterfront and Wan How's, and which seemed to him the only point upon which that boarded door could open, when suddenly a big, closed car swung into the triangular space and out of it jumped five men who, even in that light, he could not mistake but for Egyptians of exactly the same type as the unpleasant-featured Ali.

They were all, he could see clearly, of the same stocky, muscular physical build as the men in the Fortescue Square house, and moved about the car with the silent litheness of so many big cats. That they were men who could well hold their own in any sort of an affray was quite obvious. At a word from one of them, a big fellow whose face seemed to have been heavily scored by a knife or some similar lethal weapon, they all joined together and commenced jabbering in subdued tones. In the stillness of the early morning, the voices carried quite distinctly to him, but all that he could make out of their lingo was that the big fellow, who was undoubtedly their leader, was called Mustapha.

From where he had flattened himself instantly against the wall in a deep shadow, he could make each man out quite clearly, and of one thing he was positive; that none of them were any of those he had encountered at Professor Farman's house.

At a second sharp word from the big man, the jabber ceased, and they stood listening intently to what were evidently their orders for something that was to come. Suddenly, in the middle of it, the man, Mustapha, gave a quick ejaculation and pointed excitedly out to midstream. At once they started off again, but this time in excited whispers of which McCarthy could catch no word.

Following the pointing finger of the big man, the Inspector saw that from under the lee of the liner and fully under her headlights for a moment or two, a long, grey speedboat shot out and was skimming her way up river at a terrific pace.

Instantly the man, Mustapha, jumped to one of the car's headlights and, with the broad-brimmed slouch-hat he wore, began signalling by a series of long and short cut-offs of the beam. It was apparent to him that there must evidently have been a sharp look-out kept upon the flying motorboat at this spot, for she picked up the signals at once and, slowing down, began to answer them. Not a doubt but that those on the speedboat must have expected these Egyptian gentry to be where they were at that time. For what purpose?

McCarthy, watching fascinatedly, saw that they were using a signal code which must have been private and not Morse, with which he was adept—had it been the latter, he would have been considerably more interested even than he was.

For perhaps two minutes this went on, then the deep thrum of the motorboat's engines came across the water again, and she continued up river at the same amazing speed.

This interlude over, McCarthy from his watching-post saw the Egyptian cut off the headlights of the motor, and, followed by his men, cross the cobbles and enter Wan How's dive. As they passed the entrance he got an even clearer view of each of them; and the grim purpose in the ugly face of each man told its own story. If this were not a killer gang, he told himself, then never, in all his experience, had he seen one.

That Wan How had been previously notified of their coming was evident by the fact that he must have hurried to the door to meet them. McCarthy could hear his blank, oily voice just inside, though he spoke in too low a tone for the Scotland Yard man to catch his words. Gradually the voice droned away out of hearing as Wan How led his sinister-looking visitors into the room.

Thinking quickly, McCarthy gave his mind to the problem of these newcomers; these Egyptians who were evidently connected with someone ranging the river in the fastest speedboat he had ever seen in his life. What did their coming down to this den to-night portend?

Stealthily crossing to the car, he stooped and examined the numberplates and found it to be D.P. which he knew to be Reading! *Reading!* The name of the Berkshire town cleared the whole business in his mind; it opened out before him in a mental panorama. The men under Ali at Professor Farman's house and these men here with the horrific-faced Mustapha, were one and the same gang!

This particular lot were Dorasso's section, and all were engaged in the running of Egyptian opium.

But why this arrival at Wan How's? It was only too plain from the speed at which the motorboat had been dashing up the river until the signals stopped her, that no landing of any drug had been arranged for to-night. There must be some other purpose behind the visit. Others of the gang, and probably Dorasso himself, had been in the boat.

Looking back over the events of the past few hours, it seemed clear to him now that his unfortunate mention of Limehouse when he jumped from the roof of that outhouse on to the roof of Withers' cab had been heard by one or both of those men in the yard, who had reported it to the professor. Being in league, as they undoubtedly were, with Wan How, the word "Limehouse" would be instantly associated with the Chinamen who, in all possibility handled that part of the business which concerned getting the drug into the hands of the peddlers who, in turn, got it out into London and the provinces.

With it being known to all parties concerned that opium had been the subject of Grey's investigations at the time he was killed, and the professor having more than a strong suspicion that Dorasso was being sought for for that crime and also for the later killing of Fox, what more natural than for him to report to Dorasso by 'phone that an unknown man had invaded the house and discovered that there was opium in it, if nothing else? Also that the said unknown had been heard to order the driver of the car which brought him to go to Limehouse. Again McCarthy cursed himself for that slip—it had borne fruit only too quickly.

And then another thought crossed his mind, bringing with it a sudden, acute anxiety. Had, by any chance, the watching Ali seen that it was a paper which he had passed under Miss Ridley's door, and had that paper been taken from her? If such were the case, then Farman would know that it was he, McCarthy, who had raided his house and purloined his opium-pills. A thousand times more than if he were unknown would they have a motive, and good reason for having him put out of the way before he could make known what he had discovered to the authorities.

Had these Egyptians been sent from Reading to put paid to him, once and for all, and had that signal been a warning to Dorasso not to land any stuff because they knew that he, McCarthy, was there?

He was soon to be answered.

He was shaken from his thoughts by the tap of a heavy stick upon the cobbles, and turned to find the white-haired man almost at his elbow.

"Get out of this, mate, as quick as you can," he warned in a whisper, "unless you want to be carted out, feet first! That mob of Nile rats who have just come in are after you, and if they lay hands on you it's going to be a killing job, and a quick one, too. I understand their lingo as well as they do themselves, and I've been doing a bit of listening-in. They've been sent by whoever their boss is to get a Scotland Yard man by the name of McCarthy. Wan How, who's in the job up to the neck, has just told their head man that he's positive that you're the one they want. From what I could hear, he's had you followed the whole of the day, and he's open to bet any money that you're the man they're after. You know your own business best, but if you *are* him I'd vamoose out of this mighty dam' quick. Those *fellaheen* are dam' bad medicine when they start their carving antics."

"Who are they?" McCarthy asked, without troubling to either deny or confirm his identity. "Could you make out enough to say with certainty who sent them?"

"No. They mentioned no names except this McCarthy. But I can tell you that they come from up the Thames somewhere, and they're the sort that killing a white man, and particularly a Britisher, is just sheer joy to. I've handled hundreds of the swine in my time, and, damme, I know how to do it, too."

Before McCarthy could put another question to him, with a warning jerk of his stick towards the entrance he was gone.

"Now who the devil might you be?" he said to himself as he shot across the yard and to a position behind the car. "A decent sort, whoever you are!"

CHAPTER XIX

INSPECTOR MCCARTHY HAS A NARROW SQUEAK!

HIS kindly informant had scarcely disappeared into the shadow of some old riverside warehouses when one of the doors furthest from the main entrance opened and the men who had come in the car slipped out into the triangle. He saw that they were alone.

That told him two things—the first that Wan How himself must have let them out because it was a private door used only by himself and never, under any circumstances, by his patrons. As a matter of fact McCarthy knew that it led into what might be called Wan How's private suite, where he kept his singing-girls and, after certain hours, lived therein the life of an Oriental *sybarite*. The key, McCarthy had good reason for believing, was always in that pocket up Wan How's capacious left-hand sleeve.

The second, that the wily old Chinaman was going to keep his gang well out of whatever was to happen—the murder of a well-known detective would undoubtedly have sudden and extremely violent repercussions, even though the body were not found anywhere in the vicinity of his place.

The triangle was absolutely empty—it seemed almost as though everyone knew what was afoot and were making sure that, by no possible means, could they be dragged into it as witnesses or anything else. He quickly realised that any attempt to duck out of his present position would be a bad move. As it was, he was where they would least expect to find him—in the shadow of their own car. To endeavour to move into the much broader and heavier ones of the walls and towering warehouses would mean that he would have to cross a partially-lighted patch in which he could not hope to escape observation.

But these Egyptians seemed to have the facility of a cat for seeing in the dark, for, after a moment's general search, they suddenly spread out in fanlike formation which left them almost completely surrounding the car. Instantly he knew that he had been spotted.

One of the men, a fellow well to the rear of him, let out a little exultant yelp and, whipping a knife from his belt, charged directly at him. The rest of the crew closed in quickly and the right hand of every man gripped a similar weapon. As he jerked his automatic pistol from his pocket and jammed the silencer down tightly, McCarthy, almost subconsciously, noticed that such few lights as were to be seen from the exterior of Wan How's suddenly went out, leaving the place in utter darkness. The old yellow fox, he thought grimly, was going to well and truly alibi himself upon this night's foul work.

Choosing the figure of the powerful-looking Mustapha as his first target, McCarthy fired once from the hip. He was rewarded by seeing that evil-looking ruffian do a half-spin as he ran, then drop to his knees, clutching at his thigh.

Almost simultaneously, a knife flashed from the hand of one of his attackers, shaved his neck by the nth of an inch and stuck quivering in the woodwork of the car. It hummed like an angry bee.

It was then that he realised that the black square of the vehicle was, as his attackers had placed themselves, actually throwing him into relief—he would be far better off in the open.

Dodging out on to the cobbles, he narrowly missed a second knife, hurled with tremendous force, which shattered itself to pieces against a wall some thirty feet or so behind him. A snapshot he took at the thrower, but missed.

It was at this moment that, out of the corner of his eye, he caught sight of four creeping figures moving stealthily out of the alley which lay between the side of Wan How's and the river. Hatchet-men? Had the business of finishing him off taken longer than the old devil had anticipated and had he been scared into sending out his own men to end the job quickly? He had no doubt whatever that, from one or other of those black windows Wan How's wicked slit eyes were watching all that he could see.

Two shots he pumped at the newcomers and, with a little squeal of pain that went up, knew that he had hit one of them. The sound of a falling body made that much certain.

Instantly the other three opened out and ran to where the Egyptians, held for a moment by the fall of their leader, were beginning to advance upon him again.

The situation was indeed critical. Whichever angle of that triangle he worked back to, it might be only to meet another contingent of Wan How's men!

Then, suddenly—and almost as if the method had been prearranged—the seven opened out into an arc and made a concerted rush. But before he could fire, and to his intense astonishment, there came from the shadows somewhere behind him, the sound of a revolver of heavy calibre and one of them stumbled forward and pitched upon his face. An instant later the weapon sounded again and the next man flung up his hands and went down with a thud. McCarthy fired at one of the yellow men in whose hands he had caught the glint of a hatchet-head. With a choking little cough the man first sat down and then rolled over, his falling weapon striking sparks from the stones.

A voice out of the darkness bellowed into the night.

"Back, you scum, if you don't want to fill coffins!" it roared. "I know your blasted breed, and just what to do with the like of you. Get back or die! Take it or leave it! I'm not as keen on killing you as I am your boss, but it won't worry me, whichever way it goes!"

McCarthy recognised the voice as that of the white-haired man who had warned him, and instantly sent another burst of shots straight at the now petrified killers. But he fired low, having no wish to kill his men outright; he wanted them alive for the law to deal with, along with the man who employed them.

But even the effect of his low shooting demoralised the assassin gang, both yellow and brown, completely; they backed rapidly, huddled in a heap . . . and then Nemesis took them in the rear.

From around the corner, and travelling at top speed, Withers' taxi-cab came at them, as straight as ever an arrow left the bow of an English archer.

From where he was, McCarthy heard the thump of his foot as he drove his accelerator flat to the floor. Like a flying battering-ram his radiator smashed into the backs of the rear ones, sending two of them flat upon their faces with shattering force; his mudguards sent another pair flying on their skulls quite ten feet away. Then, as that unseen weapon cracked out again and one man cried out, clutching at his stomach, the others broke openly and fled into the alley by the side of Wan How's. Their car they left deserted where it stood.

Bringing his taxi to a standstill, "Big Bill" jumped out, a huge eighteen-inch spanner in hand.

"Sorry I was late, guv'nor, but I 'ad a devil of a job to git it started up at all. Strikes me, someone'd done a bit of 'anky with the car."

"And that wouldn't surprise me in the slightest, Withers," McCarthy said. "However, you can take it from me that you arrived at the best possible time you could have done—the crucial moment, with a vengeance. But for you and another unknown friend I'd have been in a devil of a jam."

Turning, he called into the darkness,

"Thanks, friend, whoever you are. Hadn't you better away with us before the rest of Wan How's 'choppers' come out and get to work?"

"You look after your own business," a gruff voice told him. "I'm well able to take care of myself against this sort of scum."

To McCarthy's amazement, the voice came from the driving-seat of the car the Egyptians had arrived in! In some mysterious way or other, and during the brief lull, the unseen shooter must have shifted his position, and darted into the car. Before McCarthy could utter another syllable, its engine roared out, it shot round in a circle and darted out of the triangle, leaving him staring out of it in a species of stupefaction.

But he realised that not a moment was to be wasted there if Withers' timely arrival was to do any good.

"Wot abaht these 'ere stiffs, or wotever they are?" that worthy wanted to know, jerking his spanner in the direction of the forms upon the ground.

"They've got what they asked for," McCarthy said coldly. "They won't get far before we get them again."

Taking his torch from his pocket and masking it, he made a brief inspection of those lying there. The yellow men he knew—they would readily be picked up later. Two of them would never need picking up, but whether he or the white haired man had shot them he neither knew or cared. As he had said, they had got what they asked for.

The man, Mustapha, tried viciously to stab at him as the light was turned into his face, but a tap upon the head from Withers' huge spanner sent him down flat again.

A sound which came from the alley had McCarthy instantly on the alert.

"Now for the round up, Withers," he cried, jumping into the cab as a low hum of voices came to him. "Nearest police station—quick. Then make for Reading and knock the last ounce of speed out of this old shandradan that she can stand!"

CHAPTER XX

IN WHICH THE NET IS DRAWN SLOWLY
AROUND MR. JUNG DORASSO!

THE manner in which Mr. William Withers piloted his ancient taxi between Wan How's and the nearest police-station was indeed masterly. Added to the speed which he knocked out of his vehicle's engine, it would have got him complete loss of licence and six months with hard labour from any stipendary magistrate before which he might have been hauled. But as the only myrmidon of the Law before whom he was ever likely to come over the matter was exhorting him to still greater illegalities, Mr. Withers cared not one tinker's damn for what the results might be.

Arrived at the station, McCarthy's orders were brief and to the point.

" 'Phone all station houses and raid Wan How's and Joe Raffi's with every man you can get on the job. Hold everyone there in custody—everyone. Cell the lot, but keep Wan How entirely by himself. Don't let him get a chance of a word to a soul once he's nabbed. Then take the damned place apart until you find opium."

He laid upon the table one of the precious pills he had taken from Farman's room.

Waiting until the Inspector-in-charge had spat through the 'phone orders that would have fifty men, on or off duty, on the run for Wan How's, he grabbed the receiver and dialled the river-police station at Wapping Old Stairs. A moment later the voice of that hard-boiled old veteran of the river-police, Inspector Tom Corrigan, assailed his ears.

"Tom," he said excitedly, "there was a magnificent grey speedboat went up the river at the devil of a pace not so long since."

"Saw her," Inspector Corrigan answered laconically. "She's often down this way at night. She belongs to someone who lives up above the bridges, somewhere."

"A dashed sight farther up than that, Tom," McCarthy said. "If you said the locks near the head of the river, you'd be nearer it. Anyhow I want her followed. Not by your tubs, of course. They're pretty smart, but they'd never get within a hundred miles of her, the way I saw her go. 'Phone on every station of the river towns to keep tab on her—Hammersmith, Kew, Richmond, Kingston, and the whole lot of 'em. Tell 'em to 'phone you at every point she passes. I'll contact with you as often as I can."

"What's the lay, Mac?" Inspector Corrigan questioned curiously. "Anything big connected to her?"

"Big!" McCarthy echoed. "The biggest thing you've ever been connected with in your lifetime, me lad. I'm on to the gang that's importing Egyptian opium—the same lot that have killed two of our best men. That grey speedboat is their drug-runner."

"Hells bells!" the Inspector gasped. "That dirty lot? Why didn't you say so before? Get off the blasted line, will you. You're obstructing me in the course of my duty. So long!"

Ringing off, McCarthy got a trunk call to Reading and issued a stream of orders to the Inspector who answered his ring.

"And don't forget," he concluded impressively. "Don't let a man of yours be seen near the house itself. Leave that to me. There is evidence there that I want to get out of the place, myself. Good-bye, till I get down."

"And how long will that take, Withers?" he questioned that bull-headed gentlemen.

"Big Bill" rubbed his prognathous chin a moment or two in thought.

"How far is it from London to Reading by way of Slough and Maiden'ead?" he inquired. McCarthy considered a minute.

"Somewhere about thirty miles, I think, Withers," he replied.

"Oh, well, say somewheres about twenty minutes," "Big Bill" said with a grin. "That's if the old jigger don't blow 'erself sky-'igh on the road," he amended cautiously.

But although Mr. Withers' rate of speed upon the road was such as to scandalise all officers of police on duty, and the nature of his driving in general of so reckless a description as to have his number hurriedly inscribed into at least half a dozen police notebooks as he flew by their owners, by some special dispensation of a benign providence, they arrived safely before the police headquarters of the Berkshire country town.

"But, mind y', Guv'nor," Mr. Withers informed his patron, "I'd lay an 'undred nicker to an 'en's egg that she won't get us back again! If she ain't tore 'er perishin' vitals out on this 'ere trip, then she ain't got none to tear, which is what I've suspected for a long time."

"If she conks out after what we'll call this 'official' run, Withers," McCarthy informed him, "we'll follow this tin bloodhound to the grave, bury her with full ceremonial rites, and interview the Chief-Commissioner, himself, upon the point of getting you a new one."

"I allus said you was a perfect gent," Mr. Withers uttered with a solemnity due to the subject, "and I don't doubt as wot 'Is 'Ighness, the Chief-Commissioner is the same. And, if so be it should 'appen that 'e does find me a new 'un, all I ask is that it ain't the same sort as this old bitch. She's bloody near worried me into the tomb, one way and another."

Upon McCarthy assuring him that he would give his best attention to this particular point, Mr. Withers heaved a sigh of relief, and observed that 'she'd make a dam' good hen-house for somebody as wasn't particular wot they 'ad at the bottom of their gardings.'

Arrived in the station, McCarthy learned that the capable Berkshire Constabulary men had been well up to their job. The house in question had been located and was already surrounded by some thirty-five men who had strict injunctions not to go within a certain radius of it and to use all possible circumspection.

The house in question was one of several that stood at considerable distance from each other on the top of that magnificently-wooded slope which runs up from the Thames to what is known locally as Caversham Heights. It stood in large, well-wooded grounds which almost completely hid it from the road, and was far from easy of access.

They had speedily discovered from local men ranging that beat that it was the residence of a certain Mr. Jung Dorasso, a wealthy Egyptian importer, who had made his headquarters in England. He dealt in rugs, carpets, and various other branches of Near-Eastern trade.

He kept an army of native servants upon the place, presumably Egyptians, though he had never been known to entertain. He had quite a fleet of cars, but spent most of his time upon the reaches of the river in his magnificent speedboat, *Cleopatra*. This appeared to be his sole hobby, and often, it was understood, he went long trips in her down below all the locks and as far as the Thames Estuary; at times penetrating as far as some of the little inlets about Foulness and the bleak, flat, Essex coast. Mr. Dorasso was not known to any of his neighbours, nor did he evince the slightest desire to become acquainted with any of them. But, the capable Inspector-in-charge informed McCarthy, he, in the interval between his ring, had searched diligently through the pages of the London directory, but could find no trace whatever of Mr. Dorasso's City or West End place of business—information which did not surprise the Scotland Yard man in the least. Dorasso's business, he thought grimly, was not one to be advertised—very far from it!

Using the telephone, he got in touch with Wapping Old Stairs, to find that Corrigan's last news of the speedboat, come in but a few moments before, was that she was negotiating the lock at Kingston on Thames.

"I can have her stopped there, Mac, if you want it," that zealous officer informed him eagerly.

"You do," McCarthy hissed through the 'phone at him, "and I'll come down to Wapping and shoot you stone dead on sight. Give orders for her to be let go straight through, but kept under watch as far as it's possible. But, mark you, don't let her see a sign of anything to make her suspicious. The first thing the man I want would do is dump his cargo and leave us all in the devil's own mess. I want to take him red-handed. You needn't trouble the Reading police—they're working in conjunction with me. That clear?"

Being assured that it was, and that his instructions would be carried out to the letter, McCarthy rang off and began to make preparations for his own part in this business. He would have liked to have had a report from the men who were on watch in Fortescue Square, but he could see no way of contacting them at that hour of the morning.

For some reason or other he had a most uneasy feeling concerning the well-being of Miss Ridley, though what was to happen to her in a house under such close observation that entrance or exit from any side was an absolute impossibility without detection, he could not see. But, still, there it was, and he would be a thankful man to see the young lady in the care of anyone else than the dope-addict, Farman.

"Well, now," he said to the Inspector, "I'm making for the house myself, and I'd be glad if you'd stand by here to take anything that comes through for me from any direction."

"If you say so, of course," the local man replied, somewhat grudgingly. "I'd rather hoped to be in at it with you, Inspector. You see," he pointed out, "I'm expecting the 'Sooper' here at any minute to take charge of our end and, after that, all the chance I'll get at the active side of it, won't be much."

"There's nothing I'd like better, Inspector," McCarthy said, "but I simply must have a man at the 'phone who can use his head while I'm away. You see, there's this speedboat to be watched like a cat, and Corrigan will be reporting in with every bit of news he gets. I can't be here and up at the house at the same time and, as I say, once she gets into your part of the river, the whole question of nabbing them red-handed, which is absolutely vital, will be up to you."

His disappointment softened by this explanation, the Inspector smiled cheerfully.

"Leave it to me," he said. "It isn't often that I get a chance at anything big. I'll handle it right enough."

"That's the lad," McCarthy said heartily, tapping him on the shoulder. "And now, is there any sort of a car handy that'll run me across Caversham Bridge?"

But it appeared that there was not—every police car was already out on the job, and they had thought, locally, that Inspector McCarthy would have been certain to have brought one of the Flying Squad cars down.

"Flying Squad car, is it?" McCarthy chuckled. "Man, if you step outside and take a view of the Flying Flea-pit that's got me here you'd never do any more good. However, it's got us this far, perhaps it can stagger on the odd mile or so."

But that Mr. Withers' outraged vehicle absolutely refused to do. No amount of cajoling or hissed objurgations on the part of its owner could get it to budge one inch. All it did upon Mr. Withers either pressing its self-starter or wielding the starting-handle strenuously, was to emit a faint whirr and a couple of clucks which might have come from a broody hen, then lapse into complete inactivity again.

"It's no good, sir," "Big Bill" bewailed. "We done the old perisher in on the run down from Town. She's conked out for the last time."

"A sort of 'Custer's Last Ride,' " McCarthy commented, then, as a sudden thought struck him, eyed the gigantic Mr. Withers suspiciously. "You haven't been giving a bit of assistance, have you?" he inquired. "Towards that new car we spoke of getting out of the Commissioner, I mean. Haven't been giving the Hand of Providence a bit of help, as you might say!"

But Mr. Withers' passionate rebuttal of any such idea so unworthy of the actions of a man and a brother towards a patron such as was Detective-Inspector McCarthy were so loud and insistent that the gentleman to which they were addressed shut him up promptly.

"By the Sainted Mike, man!" he exclaimed, "will you pipe down that voice of yours! The well-known bull of Basham couldn't make more row if he tried his damnedest. D'ye want them to hear you up on Caversham Heights? Come along, we'll do it on foot. And, in any case," he added, "should this Dorasso have the river watched, it will be better for us to approach the place that way."

CHAPTER XXI

INSPECTOR McCARTHY STRIKES MORE THAN HE BARGAINS FOR

INSPECTOR MCCARTHY, followed at some little distance by "Big Bill" Withers, crept slowly and cautiously up the steep, heavily-wooded slope from the river in the direction of Dorasso's house. More than once dark, shadowy forms had stepped out from behind trees and gave him whispered challenge. To them, McCarthy gave back a number which, by the foresight of the Inspector he had not so long since left, had been arranged with his men so that they should know exactly who they were dealing with. It was, in point of fact, a countersign for the night—or rather, early morning.

Just what they were doing on this jaunt with the crack C.I.D. "ace" the local men had no idea, nor did McCarthy intend to enlighten them. The only unofficial member of the party, Mr. Withers, was crawling some twenty feet or so in the rear of McCarthy, carrying over one shoulder a length of tow-rope which the C.I.D. man had conceived might be useful. He had brought of his own volition, and without consultation with the Inspector, his weighty eighteen-inch spanner, which, in his private opinion, might be more useful still.

On they went, until they came to a brick wall, the height of which more than suggested that if there was anything in this world Mr. Dorasso wanted it was privacy within his own demesnes.

At "Big Bill's" suggestion, McCarthy used his herculean back as a sort of ladder; from the taxi-driver's broad shoulders he could peer easily over that wall—insofar as one could peer into an almost impenetrable blackness, rendered more so by closely set trees and thick over-grown shrubs. Then, placing his hands upon the top of the wall, he vaulted over and dropped as lightly and noiselessly as a cat.

Throwing the end of his rope over the wall to the Inspector, by its aid Withers negotiated the obstacle, and did so with an agility absolutely remarkable in so ponderously-built a man.

Through the thick undergrowth of the neglected grounds, McCarthy crept as quietly as a weasel in the direction he believed the house to be situated; so far, it was not to be seen through the overgrown verdure. Then, suddenly, it loomed black and silent before them, and while they had still some twenty or thirty feet of the spinney to negotiate.

For a minute or two McCarthy knelt and surveyed the place worriedly, the horrible thought sinking through his mind that this complete and utter stillness *could* mean that Dorasso had received some warning and had passed the order on to evacuate the place instantly, destroying anything that might be in it to implicate him. Then the sharp cracking of a twig not many feet from him brought him up, rigid and motionless as a statue.

Out of the gloom came a softly-stalking figure who, at one point stood out in clear relief in the faint starlight which showed in the open space. McCarthy could not see his features, but, by his build, judged him to be another of the Egyptians. Beneath one arm he was carrying a double-barrelled breach-loader. So, Mr. Jung Dorasso had his grounds prowled at night by at least one armed guard; sure evidence that there was something to be concealed in the place, for he would certainly not preserve game on Caversham Heights.

As McCarthy watched him, the shrouded figure stooped and, by the light of a dim torch he switched on, examined something upon the ground. Then, evidently satisfied by what he saw, he moved on again with the same stealthy, sliding step.

McCarthy waited until the man was sufficiently far ahead to render movement safe, then crept towards whatever had been the object of his attention. He found it to be one of those barbarous relics of an earlier day, and now entirely forbidden by law—a man-trap! Its powerful steel, shark-like jaws were set wide open to crush the ankle and hold prisoner in horrible agony any so unfortunate as to place foot upon its spring!

McCarthy's lips compressed tightly in anger. Mr. Jung Dorasso meant crossing his grounds to be as dangerous a job as he could possibly make it. How did he know that some wretched tramp, seeking a bit of shelter and with no ulterior motive for being there at all, or, still worse, some adventurous child after fruit, would not fall victim to the damnable thing, to be maimed for life!

"Heaven knows how many of these things there are, Withers," he whispered, "or just where they've got them placed. In the most unlikely places, you can bet. For the love of Mike don't lift your feet an inch from the ground—slither them along."

"Big Bill" surveyed the horrible implement with disgust.

"Say the word, guv'nor," he whispered angrily, "and I'll go after him, give 'im a dab on the back of the neck with this 'ere spanner, and shove 'is flamin' 'ead into it!"

Restraining his follower's ardour, McCarthy motioned him to keep perfectly still. Groping until he found a tough piece of stick, he pressed it down upon the spring. Instantly the cruel jaws snapped together, shearing the wood through as though it had been so much paper and giving forth a sharp, clear clicking sound, doubly intensified by the stillness of the night.

"That will probably bring him back," he whispered, and pulled Withers into the shadow of a shrub.

"Nobody 'opes it more'n I do," Mr. Withers muttered, gripping his spanner tightly.

All at once the guard was heard returning.

"He thinks he's got a find," McCarthy whispered.

"'E 'as!" Mr. Withers muttered. "One as is goin' to do 'im a big bit o' no good at all! Let me fix 'im, guv'nor," he whispered pleadingly. "I ain't 'ad a clout at nobody to-night!"

McCarthy grinned in the darkness; he knew his Withers, and if the Egyptian did not regret making the taxi-man's acquaintance, then he, McCarthy, would be the most surprised man on earth.

"You take him, then," he whispered. "But for heaven's sake do it neatly or you may get something from that rifle of his which may put the boot on the other foot. And remember, no sound! There may be others of his sort about. I don't want any alarm raised till I've got into that house."

Suddenly the figure of the guard appeared within a few feet of them, his gun held in readiness, but, seeing or hearing nothing, he stood for a moment in indecision, then gave his attention to the closed trap. It was evident to the two watchers that he could not understand the reason for its springing and, kneeling, laid down his weapon, set it again after an effort, then examined the piece of wood which had been cleanly shorn by its jaws. Once, the piece of stick still in his hand, he peered all round him suspiciously, then Mr. Withers' spanner, hurled with unerring aim, took him exactly across the back of the neck and dropped him like a stone. The marvel was that he did not fall face downwards into the terrible instrument he had just set!

A rapid search of his pockets revealed a heavy automatic pistol of Belgian make, fully loaded and a razor-edged, ten-inch-bladed knife.

"Mr. Dorasso certainly takes precautions," McCarthy murmured.

" 'E most suttingly do," "Big Bill" agreed, "and 'ere's one of 'em 'as is come all unstuck, in a manner o' speakin'."

Pocketing the man's weapons, McCarthy broke the breech-loader open and hurled the stock one way and the double barrel the other. It would work no mischief upon this night. Pulling the filthy silk neckerchief which the Signor Sperozza invariably sported from his own neck, he bound the man's hands tightly behind him, then waited for his return to consciousness.

As this had every appearance of taking some time, his recovery was considerably accelerated by a process which "Big Bill" Withers called "giving 'is lugs a bit of a tug." How they ever remained attached to the man's head was a marvel to McCarthy after the treatment Withers gave them, but the effect was amazing. In less than a minute the man blinked his eyes, then opened them, to see in the light of the torch the two automatic pistols that were covering him steadily.

"I don't know whether you understand English or not?" McCarthy said quietly, "though I expect you do. But if you don't, it's unfortunate for you, because I'm telling you that if you utter one sound or syllable other than answer the questions I'm going to put to you, I'll blow your brains out, there and then."

The man muttered something incoherent in his own language, but it was quite evident by the deadly fear in his eyes that he understood what was being said to him.

"How many of you are there ranging these grounds?" McCarthy asked.

There was no reply, and he repeated the question.

Still no reply.

Promptly Mr. Withers caught hold of one of those lacerated ears which were now swollen considerably and of that shiny red colour generally associated with chilblains, and proceeded to go to work upon it again.

"Any questings as this 'ere gent asks of yer," he observed, "you answer 'em quick and lively, or you won't be able to 'ear when anybody else speaks to yer. Git me?"

His victim evidently did, for at once, and in fairly good English, he replied that there was only himself.

"Which might be a gag, for all we know, guv'nor," "Big Bill" interposed in a whisper. " 'E's a snide-lookin' 'ound which I wouldn't put nothink a-past, so I wouldn't. You tell 'im the fust one as shows up he'll get 'is belly blew right through 'is bleedin' 'at. Tell 'im 'e'll git it, any'ow, if 'e don't come up to scratch, suitable and proper!"

A threat, this, which had the effect of bringing from the man a startling piece of information. In an impassioned whisper, he informed them that he had had nothing to do with anything that had been going on, and particularly with regard to the lady. He had been on duty in the grounds when they had brought her in, and did not know even where she had been put or what had been done to her.

The words struck McCarthy like a physical blow. In the whole of this Egyptian opium business and the two murders for which it had been responsible, there was only one lady connected with the case in any way, and she entirely innocent of any knowledge of it—Miss Ridley! Could they have—?

"What lady is this?" he demanded viciously, seizing the man by the throat. "Out with it, if you don't want to finish here and now."

"The one that they brought in in the car early yesterday morning; the one who came from the professor's house in London."

In an instant McCarthy had yanked him to his feet and had the barrel of his automatic jammed against his heart. "You know more about this than you're telling us," he hissed sibilantly. "I'm going to give you until I count three to say just where she is and what's happened to her."

His blazing eyes fixed upon the shifty ones of the Egyptian who quailed at what he saw in them.

"One!" McCarthy snapped.

"I—I do not know," came in a whine.

"*Two!*" came from McCarthy in an icy note.

"I tell you that I—"

"*Thr . . .!*" McCarthy counted, but the man had had enough.

"She is tied up in the room beside Dorasso's! They put her there because—"

He stopped suddenly. Something in the expression of the C.I.D. man's eyes frightened him even more than his words.

"*Well!*" McCarthy rasped. "Because—what?"

Again his pistol dug deeply into the man's breast-bone.

"Because Dorasso always wanted her," the Egyptian muttered with an evil smirk. "He offered to buy her for a big price, long ago, but the professor was afraid of something and would not sell."

The words had scarcely left his lips when McCarthy was moving swiftly towards the great black shadow that was the house.

"Guv'nor!" "Big Bill" sent after him in a hoarse whisper. "Don't go rushin' ahead like that or you'll be in one o' them there traps as sure as you're breathin'—and that ain't goin' to do the lady no good—nor nobody else, either."

Realizing, even in the rage which consumed him, the wisdom of the taxi-driver's words, McCarthy pulled up and returned.

"You're quite right, Withers," he said. "That wouldn't do anyone any good—myself least of all. This gentleman will precede us. If he walks into one of those damnable things serve him right."

Protesting with more noise than McCarthy fancied, that there were no traps between there and the house, but only on the outskirts near the wall, their prisoner assured them that they were quite safe to go ahead. McCarthy, believing not one word the man uttered, nodded agreeably.

"All right," he said. "We'll take your word—you ought to know. But you'll walk in front just the same, and you know what'll happen to you if you try to raise an alarm. On second thoughts, I don't think we'll give you the chance. Gag him, Withers!"

This Mr. Withers did by the simple expedient of rooting up a large tuft of grass and stuffing it, dirt and all, in that organ when the man opened it to protest, then tied it there with a handkerchief.

"Now 'e's nice and comfortable," he remarked as, covered by two automatics, they pushed him ahead of them.

There were four of the devilish implements upon the path McCarthy would have taken, they discovered, each of them quite as deadly as the first one they had struck, and fully capable of crippling a man for life. As they came to each one, the Inspector sprang it. At last they stood upon an open space immediately at the side of the house.

"From this on, I'm working on my own, Withers," McCarthy said. "You take this lying rat and make him go the whole round of the traps with you. Should a police rush be necessary, I don't want men injured with those things. At the slightest sign of treachery, let him have it, there and then. He doesn't matter, compared with the maiming of decent policemen."

"Guv'nor," "Big Bill" assured him feelingly, "let 'im so much as blink a eye wrong, and he gets all this gun's got, right in the pantry. So if you 'ear any shootin' out 'ere you'll know that this 'ere bloke 'as gorn down wiv all 'ands, in a manner o' speakin'."

CHAPTER XXII

INSIDE DORASSO'S HOUSE!

INSPECTOR MCCARTHY, his eyes fixed upon the black mass before him, stood perfectly still until Withers had energetically poked his prisoner before him until out of sight. Then he crept swiftly over the roughish grass plot between himself and the house.

He found it much larger than it had seemed from the outskirts of the grounds, and had evidently been built without the slightest regard to cost. All along the side upon which he was were set tall ornamental french windows which opened on to a brick piazza some three feet from the ground. Creeping around the house, he found it to be much the same upon every side, except the rear, which opened on to a large courtyard surrounded by what had once been stabling, but was now garages.

He decided, after considerable thought, to break in upon the side he had first examined. For one thing, he had a getaway to think of, particularly so if he had, as he meant having, Miss Ridley in his charge. Upon that side he had a clear open run to the cover of the outer shrubbery, and he could be quite certain that he would not blunder into any of those hell-accursed man-traps.

Taking from his pocket that telescopic jemmy with which he had forced entrance into Professor Farman's house, he went to work upon one of the french windows and, in less than no time, was inside.

Closing it carefully after him, in case Withers' prisoner had lied and there were other men prowling the grounds who might spot it and raise the alarm, he made his way to the wall opposite, feeling for the door which he could not find.

Chancing his torch for a moment, he found that he was in a big, handsomely furnished room, separated by dividing-doors from another of similar size. They were partly open. Peering through, he saw that at the end of this second room was an ordinary door, to which he crept, then opened gingerly and looked into what seemed to be an enormously wide hall in which burned a very low light.

Once in that, he began to hear, though only faintly, men's voices. As they came directly from the back of the house, McCarthy decided upon first exploring the front; there was no sense in running needless risks until he had got Miss Ridley safely out of the place.

As was not unusual in houses of that size and particular formation, a broad, heavily carpeted staircase ran up to a circular,
well-shaped balcony which ran around from right and left to the
front. Upon one side or the other of this, and most probably towards
that portion of it which served the front of the house, he judged that
Dorasso would have his bedroom.

Nipping up it, he tried the doors upon the right hand side first, to
find that they were all open and the rooms empty. All of them were
furnished in the most modern and luxurious manner. It was quite
evident that they were not used by the coloured scum who served
Dorasso.

It was then that he noticed a passage which ran under a handsome arch and went the greater part of the width of the house, then
joined up with the balcony upon the opposite side. He crept quietly
into this, then came to a sudden standstill.

Further along it were the doors of two rooms which evidently
overlooked the front entrance and, leaning against the wall opposite
one of them, was a man in the *burnous* and robes of an Arab—
possibly a personal body-servant of Dorasso's. Beside him, and set
into the wall, was a lamp, the dim light of which had not been
visible for low, Oriental hangings. In the position in which the man
was lounging, his back was turned towards McCarthy, who thanked
his lucky star he had not tried the other balcony first! Had he done
so, the two must have, inevitably, come face to face.

His principal care, now, was to work with as little noise as was
possible; the totally unexpected angle caused by Miss Ridley being
prisoner there made that absolutely necessary, if only for her sake.

Jutting across the hip of the Arab McCarthy saw the curved haft
of a scimitar he evidently wore in his sash—that weighty bladed
weapon with which a Turk or an Arab can split a sheep (or a man)
with one stroke. He could have shot the fellow down with his "silenced" gun, but to get a man in the back without giving him a
chance was totally repugnant to McCarthy, even a ruffian such as
this was likely to prove. Somehow or other he must be taken by
strategy.

Drawing back behind the hangings again, he made a run-
ning-bowline in the end of the light tow-rope he had taken from
Withers, rove the other end through that, and thus created out of it
an improvised lariat. Then he crept back into the passage and advanced noiselessly until he was some ten feet behind his man.
Whirling it once round his head, McCarthy let the loop go at the
exact moment that the whistle of the rope must have caught the

man's ear, warned him of impending danger, and swung him around to see the figure behind him.

Instantly both hands dropped to his belt, one to the haft and the other to the scabbard of the scimitar—which proved to be his undoing. Had he flung his hands upward, he could easily have warded off the noose which dropped about his neck—the noose against which McCarthy instantly threw all his weight. It fastened about his throat with a jerk which, for a split-second, seemed almost to snap his neck, then the Arab, dragged completely off his balance, went to the floor with a thud.

Before he could even get his hands to his throat McCarthy was upon him—to discover the truth of the saying that the Arab is a born fighter and gives in only when consciousness leaves him. Even half choked, this particular specimen was as vicious, as slippery, and as strong as a conger eel, and, although McCarthy was on top of him, it was not until minutes of vicious punishment had been administered that the man at last rolled over upon his back with a sigh—completely unconscious.

Instantly the Inspector rose, made for the door in front of which the Arab had been watching and in which was a key.

Slipping into it, his torch instantly showed him that he had struck the right place for, stretched out upon a bed, her wrists bound to the top and her ankles to the bottom, was the slight figure of Miss Ridley, clad only in the diaphanous garment in which she had been dragged from her bedroom at the professor's house. That she was frozen with stark terror was evident by the deathly pallor of her white face and the redness of her eyes, which told of long weeping.

"All right, Miss Ridley," he whispered. "I'm here—McCarthy. You'll be out of this in no time."

The cry of utter thankfulness which broke from her lips as she realised who the newcomer was, was enough to repay the detective a hundred times over for his efforts. Swiftly untying her bonds, he set her to rub the circulation back into her wrists and ankles, and then explored what lay beyond the window which fronted her room.

He found there a broad balcony some twenty feet or so from the ground, the low parapet of which would be easy enough to scale. With the rope he could first lower her to the ground, then make it fast and follow her; the whole essence of the situation lay in speedy action.

One glance he gave at her scanty, all-revealing attire, then darted out again into the passage. Rolling the still-completely-unconscious body of the Arab over, he took from him the heavy, white, cashmere robe he wore and also the full sash which bound him at the waist and tossed them in to her. In the darkness she arrayed herself in them, and following his instructions, crept through the french windows to the balcony and there crouched behind the parapet.

For a moment, McCarthy stood undecided as to just what to do with the fallen man, but came to the conclusion that he was safe enough for such time as it would take him to make a swift dash with the girl. But he removed the scimitar and carried it with him into the other room as a precaution.

Shifting the key to the inside of the lock, he hurried to the balcony. In the circumstances he could not afford taking the time to search Dorasso's room for the gun with which he had shot Fox—if, indeed, it were there. That must be done later. And, in any case, the leader of these Egyptians had small chance of getting back into the house with the police cordon that was around it. His first thought was for the girl.

Tying the rope about her waist, he was about to help her over the parapet when the sound of a motor running swiftly around the side of the house caught his ears. He dragged her back and out of sight as a big car which seemed to be full of men dashed around into the drive to the front of the house and made for the main gates. Had McCarthy and the girl been a moment earlier, it must have been right on top of them.

Keeping sheltered until it was completely out of sight, he was again upon the point of helping her over the parapet when an interruption came from a totally different angle. From inside the house he heard shouts and what were obviously bawled threats coming nearer and nearer. A quick dart to the bedroom door showed him that the Arab was gone from the passage—he had roused the others!

Back on to the balcony, he literally forced her over, and lowered her to the ground as fast as the rope could slip through his hands. Then, half-hitching it to the rail, he followed, the smashing at the bedroom door told him that they had only managed it in time. Down on the ground, he found that, in her bare feet, she was virtually crippled by the sharp, cutting gravel of the path.

Drawing his gun and releasing the safety-catch, he whipped her up in his arms and ran for that open grass space. Somewhere out there was Withers, and behind him the cordon of Berkshire Constabulary. As he reached the edge of the rough grass, across which he knew he would have a clear run, two figures darted out from the back of the house. As he ran, McCarthy fired at one of them and the man went flat on his face!

That checked his companion for a moment; he pulled up, took aim with a rifle, and fired. McCarthy heard the whine of the heavy bullet as it passed somewhere over him and took a shot at the man, but without effect. Then, still carrying his fair burden, he raced for the copse-like fringe of the grounds in which, although daylight was now beginning to streak the sky, he knew the girl would be perfectly safe.

The man with the rifle came running on, evidently trying to get a shot at closer range and, at the same moment, a glance to the other side showed him that three or four of the men who had tried to get him in the house must have smashed the door down, precipitated themselves over the balcony, and joined in the chase. In the van of them was the now half-naked Arab, brandishing the gleaming scimitar which he had evidently recovered from the bedroom.

Turning quickly, McCarthy sent three shots into this last group, but it did not stop them; on they came and, he realised, were gaining upon him. The one solitary pursuer upon the right hand tried a shot; it whistled far too close to him for McCarthy's liking, with the girl in his arms.

Then, suddenly, and from an angle, there pounded out from the fringe of the copse, the huge figure of "Big Bill" Withers! Unnoticed by the Egyptian whose whole attention was riveted upon McCarthy and his burden, the taxi-man came on with enormous strides. Then, for an instant, he slowed down and balanced himself—McCarthy saw his arm whirl round once, and two seconds later the Arab seemed to throw a complete somersault sideways, then he was still as a fallen tree! Withers' spanner had got in its work again!

He saw "Big Bill" race to the fallen man, grab up his precious implement, then, firing the automatic he carried, make a headlong charge for the others!

"Come back, Withers," he bawled with all the strength of his lungs, but, panting as he now was, either the order did not carry, or Withers was too full of fight to obey. To save him from what seemed certain death at the hands of the man with the rifle, McCarthy pocketed his gun, took a whistle from his pocket, and blew one shrill blast upon it.

From all sides of the grounds within his sight, he saw dark figures emerge on the run and dash for the four who were Withers' objective. A moment later he was in the undergrowth and, for a moment, laid Miss Ridley down while he got back the breath that had been fast failing him.

"I can never thank you enough," she began gratefully, when he cut her off with a little laugh.

"Don't even think about it," he said. "It all came in the day's work of finding the murderer of poor Grey."

"And have you?" she asked eagerly.

"If you mean have I laid hands upon him, for the moment I have not," he told her ruefully. "But I don't think it will be long before I have the irons on the man who killed both him and Fox. It has been that infernal withered hand which blocked me in the first case; in fact it still seems to be knocking the sense out of everything."

"Withered hand?" she echoed. "What withered hand, Inspector McCarthy? You don't mean the one that Professor Farman had— his own?"

"The one that—" McCarthy began bewilderedly, then stopped and stared at her in the rapidly-growing dawn. "You don't mean to tell me that Professor Farman had a withered hand in the house?" he questioned avidly.

"Yes," she told him simply. "He has had it for years. Ever since I've known the place, at any rate. It always stood among the curios in that room into which Mr. Grey's body was taken. It was the professor's own hand, and he kept it as a memento of a time when my father's swiftness of action saved his life. He was bitten in the palm by a deadly asp, he told me, and before the poison had time to take effect, my father severed it at the wrist and saved his life."

For a still further moment McCarthy stood gasping. Those two black spots in the palm which the doctor had spotted at once as a snakebite. There was the whole story, the likely truth, instead of the cock-and-bull story of that prophecy which the professor had sprung on him and which he, blind, blatant ass that he was, had sucked in and believed. In a flash Grey's murder reconstructed itself in McCarthy's mind. Grey's interview upon the subject of Egyptian opium had been a lie. He had gone there to charge the professor and, possibly Dorasso, of being the leaders of the opium-running gang. One or other of them, or perhaps both, had murdered him, pitched him outside the door while Dorasso got away and left that hand in the square to build up the professor's cunning suggestion that Grey's murder was a mistake and that he was the intended victim.

"Well, by the Great and Sainted Mike," he groaned. " 'Tis back pounding a beat, locking up Saturday night drunks and inspecting hawker's licences that I ought to be."

But he took heart at the thought that, long before this, Professor Farman's house, as well as Wan How's dive and Joe Raffi's had been put well through the sieve.

Leaving the inmates of Dorasso's place to the Reading men, he picked up the girl again and started down the hill again for the river. At a point where a clearing opened giving the full stretch of the river from Caversham Bridge down, the grey speedboat was coming sedately along. A car, he believed the one which had just left Dorasso's house, was waiting on the Reading side of the bridge. It was evident that the dope-runner had had no warning, and remained in ignorance of what had happened at Wan How's.

The sudden appearance of "Big Bill" gave him the freedom he needed.

"Withers," he said, "pick up Miss Ridley and carry her down to the inn at the foot of the hill. Whatever you do, keep her out of sight of any in that motorboat or car until I've done my work. Someone there will doubtless lend her a pair of shoes and some clothes—they won't lose by it. Then dig up a car of some kind to get me back to Town."

"My old blighter—" Withers was beginning ruefully, but before he could get any further McCarthy was off down the hill towards the little landing-place upon the Reading side of the river towards which the *Cleopatra* was making. At her wheel he could plainly discern the figure he saw for the first time, but whom he knew now to be Mr. Jung Dorasso, the so-called Egyptian merchant.

CHAPTER XXIII

JUNG DORASSO "SQUEALS"

TO neither the men upon the incoming speedboat, or those who awaited them, was there a single soul in sight. Dawn was well advanced now, and everything visible with perfect clarity. The Reading Inspector, if he had received, as he was bound to do, further news of the motorboat after her leaving Kingston-on-Thames, had disposed of such men as he had concealed about the bridge so cleverly that even McCarthy could see no trace of them, though he was certain that they were somewhere there.

The very nonchalant demeanour of Dorasso at the wheel made McCarthy more than ever certain that the man expected no trouble at this end. Whatever risks there may have been down-river, the Egyptian evidently reckoned them left behind, once he came into the upper reaches.

Nor was there the slightest sign of nervousness or apprehension about those of the brown-skinned crew who were either in the well, or sprawled upon her snowy decks. Whatever the message which had been flashed to Dorasso from outside Wan How's, it had contained nothing to give him the slightest apprehension.

At a word from the man at the wheel, the crew began instantly to get ready for landing its cargo. McCarthy, creeping nearer and nearer to the bridge, watched the preparations going on in both the motorboat and the car which had come down to meet it, but whose bonnet, he saw, was headed towards London.

First the stern bilge-boards of the craft came up and a number of packages, evidently weighty, were placed upon the deck. In the car similar activity was taking place—flooring boards were being pulled up and evidently beneath them was a similar cache into which the packages would doubtless be transferred rapidly.

As soon as the speedboat had moored within a few feet of the car, Dorasso himself came ashore to superintend the change-over.

What McCarthy wanted was a red-handed "cop"; something that could never be squirmed out of by an eloquent K.C. counsel for the defence. Once pin the opium-running charge solidly, the motive for the murders of Grey and Fox could be nailed so solidly to Dorasso and Farman that a conviction was a stone certainty. Add to the evidence that he could put up, the attempt upon his own life by a combination of Dorasso's Egyptians and Wan How's yellow mob, and any doubts which a jury might have would be very speedily wiped out. First Grey, then Fox, and lastly himself—all three engaged in the one investigation. No; take his man with the "stuff" on him, and the rest would be easy.

From the road which led down Caversham Hill to the bridge end he could hear the steady plog-plog of a horse's hoofs. Glancing round, he saw that it was a farm milk-cart, probably upon its way to Reading Station with its cans. He let it pass him and, in a moment was over the tail-board and in the vehicle to the intense amazement of his yokel driver.

"Keep going," he ordered abruptly. "This is police business. Drive straight ahead over the bridge and, when I drop off, you keep on your way."

Half suspecting that this was some new trick of the Milk Board inspectors, the driver obeyed readily and came across the bridge at his best pace. Beyond a sharp glance from Dorasso—a glance which evidently satisfied him—no one took the slightest notice of the homely vehicle.

As he lay upon the floor of the cart, McCarthy, to the still-greater amazement of the driver, drew his automatic and quickly fed in a fresh clip.

"Now, as soon as I drop over," he whispered, "you clear as fast as that old horse can go. There'll more than likely be bullets flying about, and one of those won't do you any good, or him either."

Which was quite sufficient for the driver. The moment he saw McCarthy disappear over the tailboard his whip came out and a couple of cuts set Dobbin going at his best gallop. Nor did his driver pull up, even at a safe distance, to see what was going to happen.

Gun in hand, McCarthy ran towards the car. "Hands up, the lot of you!" he ordered. "You're under arrest!"

It was the man at the steering-wheel of the car who fired the first shot; at McCarthy's answering one, which smashed through the windscreen, he toppled limply over the wheel and lay still. Two more shots came from the side of the gang-car, and then in an instant the whole scene changed and the vicinity of Caversham Bridge seemed to be alive with running men.

For a moment Dorasso seemed stunned by the suddenness of the attack, then, realising the situation, his hand slipped under his coat to a shoulder-holster and in it appeared an automatic pistol. But before even McCarthy could cover the man who, of all of them, he wanted alive, there came a sudden and completely unexpected diversion.

A big, black car, which McCarthy recognised at once as the one that had brought the Egyptians to Wan How's, came swaying around the turn to the bridge on two wheels. With a scream of maltreated brakes it pulled up, and from it there carne a loud, report. McCarthy knew the note of that gun! It was the same which had belched forth in the triangle outside Wan How's but a few hours before. The white-haired man was at work again!

Almost simultaneously with the sound, Dorasso spun round, his gun fell from a nerveless hand, and he clutched at his shoulder and sank slowly to the ground. Before he could grab at the pistol again, McCarthy was upon him, had seized one wrist and handcuffed it to the other. He kept his foot upon the weapon until, with his man manacled, he was able to pick it up covered by a handkerchief that no finger-prints upon it might be destroyed. A glance told him that it was exactly the same calibre as the bullet which had been taken from Fox, and if this were not the actual murder-weapon, he would be a greatly surprised man.

As he placed it in his pocket, there came a concerted rush of the Reading men who, using their truncheons freely, soon battered the gang into submission. The heart for resistance seemed to have been knocked out of them when their leader went down.

A harsh voice from just behind him spun him round to find that it came from the white-haired man of Wan How's dive.

"Smart work, mate," he said with a grim chuckle, then whipped round upon Dorasso who lay staring at him as though he were gazing upon some apparition from the tomb.

"Well, Dorasso, you brown-skinned crocodile, I've caught up with you at last, have I? It's been a damned long chase, but it's worth it all to see you with the darbies on your wrists. I've prayed for this day to come, by the Lord Harry but I have! I've prayed for it as I've been flogged along under a burning sun and sand just as hot, and I've prayed for it drenched through with rain that would choke a man if he looked up at it. But I'm tough, Dorasso; tough as teak, and I've lasted it out to see my prayers answered. But the one I want is your white-livered boss, Farman, and when he meets me he can say good-bye to this earth, if I swing for it."

"You know Farman and this man, then?" McCarthy interjected quickly.

"Know 'em," the white-haired man hissed viciously. "By God I know 'em, right enough! You can stake your last shilling on that, mate. If Joe Ridley doesn't know 'em, there's no other man who does, the dirty, double-crossing rats!"

Ridley! The father of the girl at the present moment not a couple of hundred yards from where they stood.

"But you're supposed to be dead!" McCarthy, still petrified with astonishment, managed to get out. "That's the tale that Farman has told either that or kicking about somewhere on the China coast."

"China coast be damned!" Ridley answered. "Farman knew where I was, well enough. He might have thought I was dead— that's like enough, and, anyhow, the wish was father to the thought."

"Then where have you been all these years?" McCarthy asked.

"Where have I been?" Ridley answered. "Doped and sold into bondage to an Arab slave-raider. Sold again by him into an Abyssinian slave-gang. Sold by the partner who robbed me, Farman and this dirty Nile rat, Jung Dorasso, while they got away with everything that was mine. I've worked in chains and under the lash for seven years till I managed to make my escape. But, by God, I'll pay them back for what I suffered—every minute of it!"

With a snarl which might have come from the throat of a man-eating tiger he flung himself upon Dorasso and clutched him about the throat with iron hands. It took McCarthy and Withers, who had come running across the bridge at the first shot, all their strength to drag him from the Egyptian.

"Leave him to the Law, Ridley," McCarthy whispered, placatingly. "He's wanted on a murder charge, perhaps two, that he'll never get out of."

For a moment the elder man glared at them defiantly, then shrugged his shoulders.

"Right," he said resignedly. "The gallows is a death that's a dam' sight too good and clean for either of 'em, but perhaps it'll be worse to them than killing outright."

McCarthy laid his hand upon Dorasso's shoulder.

"Jung Dorasso," he said. "I arrest you for the murder of Detective Fox of the Criminal Investigation Department, and also complicity in the death, if not the actual murder, of Detective Grey, of the Special Branch, and it is my duty to inform you that anything you may say will be taken down and may be used in evidence against you."

"Then take this down," the Egyptian snarled. "I did not kill Grey. Farman did. Let him take his share of it as well as the rest of us." A cunning light came into his eyes. "Isn't there a law in this country," he asked, "that if one of a gang turns what you call King's Evidence and tells everything, he goes free?"

McCarthy looked at him contemptuously.

"You've been misinformed," he said coldly. "And if there was, it wouldn't apply to you. You're arrested upon the murder charge, without any regard to the others. You can't turn King's Evidence upon yourself. Get into that car!"

"I'll drive him and his boat's crew, mate," Ridley said, "and you can take it from me it's the sweetest job I ever had to do in my life. Sort of poetic justice, isn't it? Queer how things come round in the long run—the mills of God, like the parsons say, grind slowly, but they grind exceeding small." He gave a bitter laugh. "Dam' rum, when you come to look at it—their own car, and driven by a man they sold into something a thousand times worse than any death."

"It certainly does seem so," McCarthy said sombrely. "But, for the moment, they're only going as far as Reading Gaol. We'll bring Dorasso to Town later, though I expect he'll be tried here for the murder of Fox. I want to get back to Town, to Farman's, as quickly as ever I can."

"You don't want to get there faster than I do," Ridley snarled. "I and that lying swine have—"

He stopped short, staring at someone who was making a way across the bridge.

McCarthy, turning in the direction of his fixed, yet bewildered gaze, saw that the object upon which his eyes were riveted was Miss Sophie Ridley. Some clothes had been lent to her which obviously belonged to a young girl of perhaps sixteen and which took years off even her youthful appearance. In them she seemed little more than a child. Here, he thought quickly, was a strange encounter—this meeting of father and daughter after all these years. Truly, indeed, was truth stranger than fiction.

Steely fingers clutched at his arm.

"Mate," Ridley said hoarsely. "Who—who is that kid coming over the bridge? She—she's like someone I knew once—someone I've been searching for, ever since I got back to England."

"You've found that someone, Ridley," McCarthy said quietly. "That young lady is your daughter, Miss Sophie Ridley."

CHAPTER XXIV

DEAD MEN *DO* TELL TALES!

FOR a moment or two the hard-bitten Ridley seemed completely stunned by McCarthy's announcement; the eyes which were fixed upon the advancing girl dilated as might those of a man undergoing extreme mental shock, and there were tears in them when he turned them almost beseechingly upon his informant.

"You wouldn't lie to a man about a thing like that, mate?" he asked brokenly. "You wouldn't lie to a poor devil back from a living hell?"

"It's true," McCarthy answered, and, in brief quick whispers told him what he knew of the girl and her relations with Farman.

"The cunning dog!" Ridley hissed. "You see his idea? If ever I managed to get out of the hell he'd sold me into, he'd have pleaded that he knew nothing about it and that he'd hunted up the kid and looked after her for old time's sake. That's what he'd have said, thinking to save himself if ever I came back for the reckoning."

"It will take more than that to save him now," McCarthy said grimly. "I think it would be better, Ridley, if you walked forward and made your identity known to Miss Ridley alone. For one thing," he explained, "I'm the most softhearted goat that ever trod shoe-leather, and I wouldn't have this scum see me dropping a tear for all the money in China."

When, a few moments later, he saw the two locked in a close embrace and the tough Ridley sobbing like a child, more than ever was he glad that he had let them have the reunion entirely to themselves.

"It's not a bad old world, Withers," he commented to that worthy who also was watching the effecting scene with a certain suspicious moisture about his eyes. "Things, and good things, happen in it, and just when they're least expected. I think it would be more fitting if Mr. Ridley and his daughter drove up to Town in whatever car it is you've dug up—if any. 'Twould be a crime for anyone else to intrude.'

A sentiment with which "Big Bill" agreed thoroughly.

"But, sir," he added dubiously, "the jigger I've 'ired is damn near as bad to look at as my old 'un. Gawd knows whether she'll ever get there."

McCarthy grinned.

"Have no fear," he returned whimsically, "under your tender care and guidance she'll last as long as Fortescue Square."

In less than an hour, McCarthy, in a police-car, followed by the vehicle in which "Big Bill" drove Ridley and his daughter, arrived before the professor's house. The Inspector was out and ringing at the bell before even the plainclothes man on duty could question him as to his business.

"You can't get in here," the man began, when the Inspector cut him short.

"Chase yourself," he snapped. "McCarthy, C.I.D. And pass in the people from the other car."

Before the man had recovered from his astonishment, he was in the hall and confronting, of all people, the Assistant-Commissioner, himself, and particularly grave Sir William Haynes looked at that moment.

"Mac," he said. "Thank Heaven you're here. We're on the horns of a terrible dilemma. We've searched this place from cellar to attic and not one trace of opium can we find."

"It's here, right enough," McCarthy said positively.

Haynes shrugged his shoulders. "You'll be cleverer than we are if you can find it. I've had a squad of picked men on it all the morning, and not a sign of dope can we unearth. Opium *tackle* in plenty, but that's no crime to possess."

"It'll be found," McCarthy growled. "Where's Farman."

Haynes pointed to the door of the room to which Grey's body bad been taken.

"In there," he answered. "He's in the charge of two men. And I may tell you, Mac," he breathed in a whisper, "that he's standing on his dignity and is going to play merry blazes with everyone concerned in this raid before he's through."

McCarthy raised his eyebrows and grinned.

"Is that so?" he asked pleasantly. "Well, well! Tell me one thing, Bill?" he asked. "Did they find any at Wan How's—of the same stuff that I got here, I mean?"

"Any quantity of it," he was told. "And Raffi's as well. And quite a dozen addicts smoking it in Wan How's cellars."

"Then it'll be found here," McCarthy said finally. "As sure as you're living, Bill, this is the clearing-house for the bulk stuff. You'd better come in with me and witness this arrest."

As he turned to the door, his eyes caught the figures of Ridley and his daughter standing in the hall.

"By the way, Bill," he said, "you'd better meet Mr. Joseph Ridley and his daughter. He's got a pretty story to tell about Professor Farman. Perhaps you'd like to see your old partner, Ridley?"

The glint that came into the white-haired man's eyes was far more eloquent than any words.

"Only, mind you," McCarthy cautioned, "no funny business. He's the property of the Law, and, as far as anything possibly can, it will avenge you."

"I'm satisfied," Ridley said quietly. "I've found my girl, who I'd given up hope of ever seeing again, and I'm satisfied. Let the Law he's laughed at so long deal with him."

McCarthy turned to Haynes.

"Give me the warrant, Bill."

With the utmost dubiousness the Assistant-Commissioner handed it over.

"For the Lord's sake be careful what you're doing, Mac, or you'll land us into the devil of a jam. I tell you again, there's not a thing to be found here. If you add a murder charge to the other—"

"That's just the very thing I'm going to do," McCarthy said shortly and led the way into the room.

At his appearance Professor Farman arose from the chair in which he had been seated, a plain-clothes man standing at each side of him.

"Inspector McCarthy," he began impressively, "in the strongest possible manner I protest against this outrage. I shall at once—"

"Tell it to the judge and jury," McCarthy said shortly. "Professor Farman, I have a warrant for your arrest upon the charge of complicity in, if not being the actual murderer of, Detective-Inspector Grey, of the Special Branch of the Criminal Investigation Department. Dorasso has squealed and charges you with the crime. It is my duty to warn you that anything you may say will be taken down and may be used in evidence against you." He nodded to one of the plain-clothes men. "Put the handcuffs on him," he ordered.

"Before you're taken away, Professor," he resumed, "there's an old friend of yours who would like very much to see you in the position in which you now stand. Perhaps you remember Mr. Ridley?"

As the white-haired man stepped out, Farman's jaw sagged and his whole body wilted.

"Ridley!" he gasped. "You!"

"You didn't expect to see me again, did you?" Ridley said quietly. "There was a time, and not so long since, when I never expected to see you again, either. But I kept on praying and hoping, and here I am. It's a great sight—both you and Dorasso with the bracelets on, and I've only one thing to say and that is that you're damned lucky to be in the clutches of the Law, both of you. For if you'd fallen into my hands, I'd have paid you with a dose of what you sold me into, and hanging's better than that."

One desperate effort Farman made to retrieve his position.

"But, McCarthy, that hand of mine! The one that was sent to me in warning. That proves I, too, was threatened by the same people who—"

"Who killed Grey?"McCarthy finished for him. "Well, now, about that hand. That is your story—Dorasso's is quite different. So is Miss Ridley's."

He turned to Ridley.

"Perhaps you could give us some particulars as to just how the professor lost that missing hand of his, Mr. Ridley?"

"Only too true, I can," Ridley answered bluntly. "He was bitten by an asp while we were opening up tombs at Asmara. He'd have been a goner if I hadn't lopped it off on a stone with a scimitar. Worst day's work I ever did. He always travelled it with him—got the idea that if ever it went out of his possession his luck would finish."

"And it *did* go out of your possession, Professor," McCarthy said softly, "for just the few minutes between Dorasso, on your instructions, dropping it in the square and the policeman finding it and bringing it back here. And in those few minutes your luck ended! You were right enough about that. Take him away! Finger-print his other hand and compare his 'dabs' with those on the haft of that knife."

The evil glance which the professor threw at McCarthy as he left the room told sufficiently what he knew would be the result of that comparison.

"And still, Mac," Bill Haynes said, a little later, "we're no nearer to finding the opium that you're so certain he has got stored here."

"What's that?" Ridley asked, overhearing the remark. "Can't find Farman's opium cache? Well, unless he's changed his methods, it's staring you right in the face."

He stepped up to the hideous-faced mummy in the hall, felt at the back of its case for a moment, and evidently pressed upon a hidden spring. The whole front of the case swung out upon invisible hinges. Inside it was the closely-swathed figure of the dead ancient.

"You'll notice," Ridley pointed out drily, "that the body hasn't shrunk much in a few thousand years. They don't when Farman gets 'em. I'll show you why."

Taking a knife from his pocket and opening the blade, he hacked at the swathings around the ribs for a moment or two, then thrust his hand into the aperture made and produced a couple of large balls wrapped in soft lead.

"There it is," he said. "Pure Egyptian opium, ready for breaking down. Open up as many of these things as he's got and you'll find the same in all of them. It takes an old partner to know a man's tricks."

It was as McCarthy and Haynes were being driven back to the Yard that the Assistant-Commissioner offered his sincere congratulations to his friend.

"You've done a dashed fine day's work for yourself, Mac," he said. "Nothing can stop promotion after this—to say nothing of adding handsomely to the exchequer. As you know, there is a three thousand pounds reward covering this lot."

McCarthy shrugged his shoulders;

"Which would be splendid if I happened to have earned it, Bill, but, unfortunately, I haven't."

Haynes stared at him puzzledly.

"What d'ye mean by that?" he demanded.

"Simply this," McCarthy answered with a sad shake of his head. "If it hadn't been for the information little Miss Ridley gave me, to the effect that Farman's withered hand had always been in his possession, I should never have joined him up with the murder of Grey. Even if Dorasso had squealed, as he did, his evidence would have come much later than that. She really nailed Farman. You can see that? Damme, it's staring you in the face."

"Yes," Haynes admitted dubiously.

"Well, that's five hundred quid of the first one thousand gone west so far as I'm concerned. It belongs to Miss Ridley."

"But," Haynes protested, "you can't—"

"I seem to remember," McCarthy interposed reminiscently, "that when I landed back from Reading, you had a devil of a mouthful to bellyache that no opium could be found in Farman's house, and I also recollect that, even after Farman was arrested for murder, you were still at the same game, telling me things in mournful numbers, so to speak. Did I really see, or was it only imagination, a certain Mr. Joseph Ridley show us exactly where Farman's bulk opium was stored and where it would certainly never have occurred to you, or me, or anyone of us, to look for it. Anyhow, your searchers hadn't. That's right, isn't it?"

"I suppose it is," Haynes admitted.

"You know damn' well it is, and that's another two thousand of the reward gone," McCarthy said placidly. "What was it offered for, Bill? That part of it?"

"For information which led to the discovery of the main hiding-place of Egyptian opium in this country, with evidence leading to the conviction of the persons implicated therein," Haynes said.

"Right. And but for Ridley producing the goods, could you have arrested Farman as a person implicated? Of course you couldn't; that's what you were bellyaching about. So that's the two thousand it's your job to see goes to Ridley. Out of the remaining five hundred," McCarthy went on before the Assistant-Commissioner could get in a word, "there's a new taxi-cab due to Mr. William. Withers, the bull-headed gentleman who is driving Mr. Ridley and his daughter. Last night he dished his own up properly in the Sacred Cause of Law and Order."

"Of all the damned fools ever I've met," Haynes was beginning, almost savagely, when McCarthy stopped him with a grandiloquent wave of his hand.

"I know what I am without you telling me," he said sadly. "And, what's worse, neither pills nor potions will cure me. But if you think I'm the sort of chap who's going to take money out of the pocket of a man who has suffered as Ridley has, and who was to start all over again in life with a beautiful young girl like his newly-found daughter to look after, you're wrong to blazes. Besides," he added whimsically, "I've plenty of money of my own; the magnificent salary I'm paid for the suppression of crime in all its branches is more than I know what to do with."

A sudden depressing thought occurred to him; one that filled him with dismay.

"By the Sainted Mike!" he exclaimed. "I mustn't forget that I owe the 'Sooper' a quid! Another short week!"

THE END

RAMBLE HOUSE's

HARRY STEPHEN KEELER WEBWORK MYSTERIES

(RH) indicates the title is available ONLY in the RAMBLE HOUSE edition

The Ace of Spades Murder
The Affair of the Bottled Deuce (RH)
The Amazing Web
The Barking Clock
Behind That Mask
The Book with the Orange Leaves
The Bottle with the Green Wax Seal
The Box from Japan
The Case of the Canny Killer
The Case of the Crazy Corpse (RH)
The Case of the Flying Hands (RH)
The Case of the Ivory Arrow
The Case of the Jeweled Ragpicker
The Case of the Lavender Gripsack
The Case of the Mysterious Moll
The Case of the 16 Beans
The Case of the Transparent Nude (RH)
The Case of the Transposed Legs
The Case of the Two-Headed Idiot (RH)
The Case of the Two Strange Ladies
The Circus Stealers (RH)
Cleopatra's Tears
A Copy of Beowulf (RH)
The Crimson Cube (RH)
The Face of the Man From Saturn
Find the Clock
The Five Silver Buddhas
The 4th King
The Gallows Waits, My Lord! (RH)
The Green Jade Hand
Finger! Finger!
Hangman's Nights (RH)
I, Chameleon (RH)
I Killed Lincoln at 10:13! (RH)
The Iron Ring
The Man Who Changed His Skin (RH)
The Man with the Crimson Box
The Man with the Magic Eardrums
The Man with the Wooden Spectacles
The Marceau Case
The Matilda Hunter Murder
The Monocled Monster

The Murder of London Lew
The Murdered Mathematician
The Mysterious Card (RH)
The Mysterious Ivory Ball of Wong Shing Li (RH)
The Mystery of the Fiddling Cracksman
The Peacock Fan
The Photo of Lady X (RH)
The Portrait of Jirjohn Cobb
Report on Vanessa Hewstone (RH)
Riddle of the Travelling Skull
Riddle of the Wooden Parrakeet (RH)
The Scarlet Mummy (RH)
The Search for X-Y-Z
The Sharkskin Book
Sing Sing Nights
The Six From Nowhere (RH)
The Skull of the Waltzing Clown
The Spectacles of Mr. Cagliostro
Stand By—London Calling!
The Steeltown Strangler
The Stolen Gravestone (RH)
Strange Journey (RH)
The Strange Will
The Straw Hat Murders (RH)
The Street of 1000 Eyes (RH)
Thieves' Nights
Three Novellos (RH)
The Tiger Snake
The Trap (RH)
Vagabond Nights (Defrauded Yeggman)
Vagabond Nights 2 (10 Hours)
The Vanishing Gold Truck
The Voice of the Seven Sparrows
The Washington Square Enigma
When Thief Meets Thief
The White Circle (RH)
The Wonderful Scheme of Mr. Christopher Thorne
X. Jones—of Scotland Yard
Y. Cheung, Business Detective

Keeler Related Works

A To Izzard: A Harry Stephen Keeler Companion by Fender Tucker — Articles and stories about Harry, by Harry, and in his style. Included is a compleat bibliography.

Wild About Harry: Reviews of Keeler Novels — Edited by Richard Polt & Fender Tucker — 22 reviews of works by Harry Stephen Keeler from *Keeler News*. A perfect introduction to the author.

The Keeler Keyhole Collection: Annotated newsletter rants from Harry Stephen Keeler, edited by Francis M. Nevins. Over 400 pages of incredibly personal Keeleriana.

Fakealoo — Pastiches of the style of Harry Stephen Keeler by selected demented members of the HSK Society. Updated every year with the new winner.

RAMBLE HOUSE's OTHER LOONS

The Organ Reader — A huge compilation of just about everything published in the 1971-1972 radical bay-area newspaper, *THE ORGAN.*

Old Times' Sake — Short stories by James Reasoner from Mike Shayne Magazine

Freaks and Fantasies — Eerie tales by Tod Robbins, collaborator of Tod Browning on the film FREAKS.

Four Jim Harmon Sleaze Double Novels — *Vixen Hollow/Celluloid Scandal, The Man Who Made Maniacs/Silent Siren, Ape Rape/Wanton Witch* and *Sex Burns Like Fire/Twist Session.* More doubles to come!

Marblehead: A Novel of H.P. Lovecraft — A long-lost masterpiece from Richard A. Lupoff. Published for the first time!

The Compleat Ova Hamlet — Parodies of SF authors by Richard A. Lupoff – New edition!

The Secret Adventures of Sherlock Holmes — Three Sherlockian pastiches by the Brooklyn author/publisher, Gary Lovisi.

The Universal Holmes — Richard A. Lupoff's 2007 collection of five Holmesian pastiches and a recipe for giant rat stew.

Four Joel Townsley Rogers Novels — By the author of *The Red Right Hand: Once In a Red Moon, Lady With the Dice, The Stopped Clock, Never Leave My Bed*

Two Joel Townsley Rogers Story Collections — Night of Horror and Killing Time

Twenty Norman Berrow Novels — *The Bishop's Sword, Ghost House, Don't Go Out After Dark, Claws of the Cougar, The Smokers of Hashish, The Secret Dancer, Don't Jump Mr. Boland!, The Footprints of Satan, Fingers for Ransom, The Three Tiers of Fantasy, The Spaniard's Thumb, The Eleventh Plague, Words Have Wings, One Thrilling Night, The Lady's in Danger, It Howls at Night, The Terror in the Fog, Oil Under the Window, Murder in the Melody, The Singing Room*

The N. R. De Mexico Novels — Robert Bragg presents *Marijuana Girl, Madman on a Drum, Private Chauffeur* in one volume.

Four Chelsea Quinn Yarbro Novels featuring Charlie Moon — *Ogilvie, Tallant and Moon, Music When the Sweet Voice Dies, Poisonous Fruit* and *Dead Mice*

The Green Toad — Impossible mysteries by Walter S. Masterman – More to come!

Two Hake Talbot Novels — *Rim of the Pit, The Hangman's Handyman.* Classic locked room mysteries.

Three Agent 0008 Novels by Clyde Allison — Sexy James Bond parodies by William Knoles. *Gamefinger, Sadisto Royale* and *Our Man from Sadisto*

Two Alexander Laing Novels — *The Motives of Nicholas Holtz* and *Dr. Scarlett,* stories of medical mayhem and intrigue from the 30s.

Three Wade Wright Novels — *Echo of Fear, Death At Nostalgia Street* and *It Leads to Murder,* with more to come!

Four Rupert Penny Novels — *Policeman's Holiday, Policeman's Evidence, Lucky Policeman* and *Sealed Room Murder,* classic impossible mysteries.

Five Jack Mann Novels — Strange murder in the English countryside. *Gees' First Case, Nightmare Farm, Grey Shapes, The Ninth Life, The Glass Too Many.*

Six Max Afford Novels — *Owl of Darkness, Death's Mannikins, Blood on His Hands, The Dead Are Blind, The Sheep and the Wolves* and *Sinners in Paradise* by One of Australia's finest novelists.

Five Joseph Shallit Novels — *The Case of the Billion Dollar Body, Lady Don't Die on My Doorstep, Kiss the Killer, Yell Bloody Murder, Take Your Last Look.* One of America's best 50's authors.

Two Crimson Clown Novels — By Johnston McCulley, author of the Zorro novels, *The Crimson Clown* and *The Crimson Clown Again.*

The Best of 10-Story Book — edited by Chris Mikul, over 35 stories from the literary magazine Harry Stephen Keeler edited.

A Young Man's Heart — A forgotten early classic by Cornell Woolrich

The Anthony Boucher Chronicles — edited by Francis M. Nevins
Book reviews by Anthony Boucher written for the *San Francisco Chronicle,* 1942 – 1947. Essential and fascinating reading.

Muddled Mind: Complete Works of Ed Wood, Jr. — David Hayes and Hayden Davis deconstruct the life and works of a mad genius.

Gadsby — A lipogram (a novel without the letter E). Ernest Vincent Wright's last work, published in 1939 right before his death.

My First Time: The One Experience You Never Forget — Michael Birchwood — 64 true first-person narratives of how they lost it.

The Incredible Adventures of Rowland Hern — Rousing 1928 impossible crimes by Nicholas Olde.

Slammer Days — Two full-length prison memoirs: *Men into Beasts* (1952) by George Sylvester Viereck and *Home Away From Home* (1962) by Jack Woodford

Beat Books #1 — Two beatnik classics, *A Sea of Thighs* by Ray Kainen and *Village Hipster* by J.X. Williams

Murder in Silk — A 1937 Yellow Peril novel of the silk trade by Ralph Trevor

Invaders from the Dark — Classic werewolf tale from Greye La Spina

Fatal Accident — Murder by automobile, a 1936 mystery by Cecil M. Wills

The Devil Drives — A prison and lost treasure novel by Virgil Markham

Dr. Odin — Douglas Newton's 1933 potboiler comes back to life.

The Chinese Jar Mystery — Murder in the manor by John Stephen Strange, 1934

The Julius Caesar Murder Case — A classic 1935 re-telling of the assassination by Wallace Irwin that's much more fun than the Shakespeare version

West Texas War and Other Western Stories — by Gary Lovisi

The Contested Earth and Other SF Stories — A never-before published space opera and seven short stories by Jim Harmon.

Tales of the Macabre and Ordinary — Modern twisted horror by Chris Mikul, author of the *Bizarrism* series.

The Gold Star Line — Seaboard adventure from L.T. Reade and Robert Eustace.

The Werewolf vs the Vampire Woman — Hard to believe ultraviolence by either Arthur M. Scarm or Arthur M. Scram.

Black Hogan Strikes Again — Australia's Peter Renwick pens a tale of the outback.

Don Diablo: Book of a Lost Film — Two-volume treatment of a western by Paul Landres, with diagrams. Intro by Francis M. Nevins.

The Charlie Chaplin Murder Mystery — Movie hijinks by Wes D. Gehring

The Koky Comics — A collection of all of the 1978-1981 Sunday and daily comic strips by Richard O'Brien and Mort Gerberg, in two volumes.

Suzy — Another collection of comic strips from Richard O'Brien and Bob Vojtko

Dime Novels: Ramble House's 10-Cent Books — *Knife in the Dark* by Robert Leslie Bellem, *Hot Lead* and *Song of Death* by Ed Earl Repp, *A Hashish House in New York* by H.H. Kane, and five more.

Blood in a Snap — The *Finnegan's Wake* of the 21st century, by Jim Weiler and Al Gorithm.

Stakeout on Millennium Drive — Award-winning Indianapolis Noir — Ian Woollen.

Dope Tales #1 — Two dope-riddled classics; *Dope Runners* by Gerald Grantham and *Death Takes the Joystick* by Phillip Condé.

Dope Tales #2 — Two more narco-classics; *The Invisible Hand* by Rex Dark and *The Smokers of Hashish* by Norman Berrow.

Dope Tales #3 — Two enchanting novels of opium by the master, Sax Rohmer. *Dope* and *The Yellow Claw.*

Tenebrae — Ernest G. Henham's 1898 horror tale brought back.

The Singular Problem of the Stygian House-Boat — Two classic tales by John Kendrick Bangs about the denizens of Hades.

Tiresias — Psychotic modern horror novel by Jonathan M. Sweet.

The One After Snelling — Kickass modern noir from Richard O'Brien.

The Sign of the Scorpion — 1935 Edmund Snell tale of oriental evil.

The House of the Vampire — 1907 poetic thriller by George S. Viereck.

An Angel in the Street — Modern hardboiled noir by Peter Genovese.

The Devil's Mistress — Scottish gothic tale by J. W. Brodie-Innes.

The Lord of Terror — 1925 mystery with master-criminal, Fantômas.

The Lady of the Terraces — 1925 adventure by E. Charles Vivian.

My Deadly Angel — 1955 Cold War drama by John Chelton

Prose Bowl — Futuristic satire — Bill Pronzini & Barry N. Malzberg .

Satan's Den Exposed — True crime in Truth or Consequences New Mexico — Award-winning journalism by the *Desert Journal*.

The Amorous Intrigues & Adventures of Aaron Burr — by Anonymous — Hot historical action.

I Stole $16,000,000 — A true story by cracksman Herbert E. Wilson.

The Black Dark Murders — Vintage 50s college murder yarn by Milt Ozaki, writing as Robert O. Saber.

Sex Slave — Potboiler of lust in the days of Cleopatra — Dion Leclercq.

You'll Die Laughing — Bruce Elliott's 1945 novel of murder at a practical joker's English countryside manor.

The Private Journal & Diary of John H. Surratt — The memoirs of the man who conspired to assassinate President Lincoln.

Dead Man Talks Too Much — Hollywood boozer by Weed Dickenson

Red Light — History of legal prostitution in Shreveport Louisiana by Eric Brock. Includes wonderful photos of the houses and the ladies.

A Snark Selection — Lewis Carroll's *The Hunting of the Snark* with two Snarkian chapters by Harry Stephen Keeler — Illustrated by Gavin L. O'Keefe.

Ripped from the Headlines! — The Jack the Ripper story as told in the newspaper articles in the *New York* and *London Times*.

Geronimo — S. M. Barrett's 1905 autobiography of a noble American.

The White Peril in the Far East — Sidney Lewis Gulick's 1905 indictment of the West and assurance that Japan would never attack the U.S.

The Compleat Calhoon — All of Fender Tucker's works: Includes *The Totah Trilogy, Weed, Women and Song* and *Tales from the Tower,* plus a CD of all of his songs.

RAMBLE HOUSE

Fender Tucker, Prop.

www.ramblehouse.com   fender@ramblehouse.com

318-455-6847   443 Gladstone Blvd.   Shreveport LA 71104

44393948R00091

Made in the USA
Lexington, KY
29 August 2015